A MOST MALICIOUS MESSENGER

KATHERINE BLACK

For T & R
The ones I love the most.

CHAPTER ONE

AIN'T THAT PECULIAR

The first time it happened, no one took much notice. A group of yummy mummies were having coffee in the room at the back of the bookshop, prams in a protective circle like covered wagons on the prairie, jackets stacked over the backs of chairs and hanging from the handles of strollers. Betty Danvers and Jean Drysdale were sipping coffee in the corner, cooing over the pink-cheeked babies hunched in their prams and the toddlers who were wobbling about. Danny Fox was tapping away on his laptop in an armchair. Bastian sat on a high stool behind the counter, discussing the upcoming Easter promotion with May, while more customers browsed in the stacks. The thump of a hoover could be heard in Bastian's flat overhead.

It was the Monday morning before Easter Sunday when everyone was gearing up for the busyness of the upcoming Easter break.

May's phone pinged first, immediately followed by a series of dings and buzzes throughout the shop. The miniature dachshunds, Bess and George, raised their heads from their cushion beside the radiator. May looked down at her phone screen. A message from an unknown number said:

> Some rise by sin. I know all about the unnatural acts you commit with your manservant. DP

She looked around the bookshop, wondering who'd sent the message. Everyone had their phones out, comparing screens and glancing around the room in confusion.

Bastian picked up his own phone. 'Did you just get an odd message?'

May nodded then leaned forward to look at Bastian's screen. They were sent the same strange text. Probably teenagers playing a silly prank.

'Definitely no concern of mine,' May said, tucking a lock of white hair behind one ear, 'as I don't have a manservant and haven't committed an unnatural act in decades.'

'Well... I don't have a manservant.' Bastian chuckled.

Sebastian Lovelace, though a mere four and a half feet tall, was known for his popularity with the ladies. May had hired him to manage the bookshop because he was enthusiastic and competent. The fact that he was one of the most handsome men she'd ever met had nothing to do with it. At least, that's what she told herself.

'Shakespeare,' Bastian said. 'The first bit, anyway.' He shrugged and put his phone face down on the desk.

The yummy mummies were aflutter, discussing the odd text until one of the toddlers decided she'd had enough and started shouting for her potty. Phones were swiftly tucked away as the group stood, gathering toys and bits of biscuit from the floor.

May and Bastian finalised the details of their stall on the heath for the church's Easter fête (take all the Agatha Christies, leave the signed first editions in the shop), then May collected her dachshunds and headed home. The dogs pranced ahead on their leads as May traipsed across the glorious heath. The grass was an abundant green, the air fresh after a recent mowing. She raised her face to the sun and inhaled deeply. Looking across at her house, Greenway, she sighed as the familiar feeling of dread settled in her chest. May had been born in the big Georgian house, had gone through phases of loving and hating the place, but had most recently been very happy there. That is, until her mother arrived.

Araminta Morrigan was ninety-six, though she insisted on telling everyone she was eighty-nine.

'Ninety-six sounds so ancient,' she would say.

'But eighty-nine makes you a mere maiden?' May would retort.

Minty, as she was called, had returned to Greenway to die. She wasn't ill, just *done*. She demanded that May help her, insisted that May would know what to do because of her long experience of killing people. It was disturbing to hear her mother say such things. How on earth did Minty know?

May had been through a difficult few years. She'd nursed her husband, James, through two years of cancer treatment. Once he'd received the all-clear, he'd thanked her for her decades of love and devotion by leaving her for another woman. Deserting her after forty years together. She'd been devastated.

That's when Fletcher, her oldest and dearest friend, had come to live with her. The two had met at Cambridge in the sixties and been friends ever since. Together, they'd managed to reclaim some of the fun of their youth. Recently, May and Fletcher had started having real adventures again. She'd been happier than she had in years.

Then Minty came home.

'Halloo, May!' Geoffrey Crichton, May's next-door neighbour, was bombing towards her across the grass on a pair of skate skis, arms flailing, poles pointing in all directions. May calmly stepped back to tuck a strand of hair under her beret, allowing Geoffrey, aka The Cretin to shoot past with his bulldog, Winston, trundling behind him.

In the last few months, Geoffrey, a rising MP, had fully embraced social media. He'd decided to be a modern politician, someone who truly connected with his constituents. At least online. Unfortunately, he'd also embraced social media ads. Lately, he seemed to be enamoured with a different gadget or product every time May encountered him. He'd started wearing a glucose monitor, though he wasn't diabetic or even borderline diabetic, and insisted on reporting his current glucose level at any opportunity. He was taking special vitamins ('completely cured my hay fever', though his pink eyes and runny nose said differently), wearing bamboo underpants ('so soft *and* environmentally friendly'), using soap created especially for men, had purchased a pair of socks with Winston's face printed on them, and subscribed to an eye-wateringly expensive paleo meal delivery service ('a gamechanger'). May assumed the skate skis were part of some new ad campaign. It was only a matter of time before The Cretin started enthusing about AI and cyber currencies.

Once safely in the wide entry hall of Greenway, she knelt to unleash the dogs, flinching at the pain in her hip. Her sciatica was improving with regular exercise, but kneeling down like this was still a challenge at times. Fletcher came to meet her in the hall, eyes agog, face flushed.

Uh-oh.

'She's wearing my Chanel bouclé jacket,' he hissed, clearly outraged. 'The bouclé, for God's sake!'

Minty had taken to helping herself to Fletcher's clothes, or rather Barb's clothes. Fletcher's alter ego, Barbara Bouvier, romance novelist extraordinaire, possessed an elegant, luxurious wardrobe that obviously appealed to the discerning Minty.

Without stopping to remove her jacket, May went straight to the downstairs sitting room that Minty had converted into her own bedroom. She was ensconced in an armchair by the window, feet dangling above the Turkish rug, reading a copy of *Vogue* while wearing the pink jacket, which was a special favourite of Barb's because it was a match for the famous Jackie O suit. Minty, rather than looking sophisticated in the haute couture ensemble, looked more like ET in the scene where the children dress him up for Halloween. Right down to the ridiculous blonde wig.

'Minty,' May said. 'I've asked you more than once to please not go through Barb's things. That jacket does not belong to you.'

Looking at May with her doll-like eyes, made larger with lavish use of eyeliner and false lashes, Minty appeared confused. 'I don't know what you mean, dear,' she said. 'By the way, I've spoken to that nice vicar at the church about my funeral. He wasn't enthused about some of my music choices, but he came round in the end.'

May rolled her eyes. Minty brought out the adolescent in her. 'You're not dying,' she said.

'And whose fault is that?' Minty replied, giving May a sour look. 'At my age, you never know. I could go at any moment. Faster, if you'd pull your finger out and get it done. Better to organise it now than end up with "Jerusalem" or "Abide With Me".' She shuddered in disgust.

'Right,' May replied. Refusing to take Minty's bait, she steered the conversation back to the topic at hand. One of Minty's favourite tactics was distraction. 'Just stay out of Barb's things from now on.'

Minty looked around the room in sudden panic. 'Where am I?' She looked at May. 'Who are you?'

'For God's sake.' May rolled her eyes again. 'You don't have dementia, you daft old bat. Stop that nonsense.'

'You know,' Minty said, slowly turning the pages of the magazine in her lap, 'I can see your lips moving but all I hear is quack, quack, quack.' She opened and shut one heavily beringed hand like the bill of a duck. 'It's the oddest thing.'

May swallowed a scream. She closed her eyes for a moment, before making another attempt to focus on her reason for entering Minty's domain. 'Just stop wearing Barb's clothes and put that jacket back where you found it.'

'Perhaps you'd like to wrestle me for it?' Minty responded, as she looked up at May. 'No? Thought not. I'd ruin you.' She looked back down at the magazine. 'Ah, here's a new contraption for removing facial hair. I'll mark this for you,' she said, turning down the corner of the page. 'In that hat you look just like David Niven in *The Guns of Navarone*, moustache and all.'

May turned on her heel and left the room.

Fletcher was in the kitchen pouring shots of tequila.

'It's not even noon,' May said, ripping the beret from her head and chucking it onto the kitchen table.

'And?' He shrugged, holding up a dish laid with little mounds of Maldon sea salt and lime wedges. 'This is medicinal.'

May surreptitiously touched her upper lip. Damn it. Minty was right.

She sighed then flicked her tongue across the base of her thumb and sprinkled the damp patch with salt. She licked the salt away, downed a shot, then sucked on a wedge of lime.

Exhaling from her toes up, May slammed the little glass down on the kitchen side. 'I needed that,' she said. 'What are we going to do about her?'

'I think you should just kill her and get it over with,' Fletcher said, as he poured another shot. 'It's what she wants. It's why she came back.' Fletcher had only recently learned of May's unusual proclivity but had come to embrace it wholeheartedly.

May shook her head. 'I'm not going to kill my own mother. Don't be ridiculous. Why don't you do it if you're so keen?'

'You're not suddenly growing a conscience, May Morrigan?' He downed his second shot of tequila, closing one eye in a grimace as he bit into the sour lime.

'This is different. She may be an irritating, demanding, malevolent little troll, but she's still my mother. Matricide is not my style.' Placing her glass in the deep kitchen sink, she looked out the window. The daffodils were flourishing, and the small cherry tree was full of blossom. Would Minty still be there when the hydrangeas were in bloom? The very thought sent a chill down May's spine.

'How were things at the shop?' Fletcher asked.

'Fine,' May said. Then, remembering the odd text, she fished around in her trusty Hermès Kelly handbag and found her mobile. 'Look at this. Loads of people received the same message.'

Fletcher read the text and tutted in response. 'Someone's up in arms about things that don't concern them,' he said.

May put the phone back in her bag. 'It seems bigots never rest,' she said. She retrieved her glass from the sink and held it out for another shot. 'What miserable lives they must lead.'

The next time it happened, someone was already dead.

CHAPTER TWO

IT'S BEEN A LONG, LONG TIME

Minty thought that perhaps she shouldn't have returned to Greenway.

She could hear the two of them in the kitchen moaning about her. She might have been forced to resort to dentures years ago, and she did have a tendency to wee herself a little bit when she coughed or sneezed or laughed too hard (well, who didn't?) but there was nothing wrong with her hearing. May and Fletcher were chattering to each other, punctuated by the occasional sound of a glass being slammed down on the kitchen side.

Tequila, she assumed. They'd always been fond of their shots.

Minty sighed and adjusted the sleeves of the Chanel jacket. It was far too large for her, really not her style at all, but she knew that it would irritate Fletcher if she took it, which would in turn irritate May. Would she be able to push May far enough to finally put Minty out of her persistent misery?

She clasped the large gold locket that was always around her neck. Originally an ornate piece, it was now worn almost smooth from handling. She caressed it between finger and thumb, the cold metal standing in for the warm man it represented. There was no need to open it to look at the faded photograph inside. His image was etched into her memory, his ghost her constant companion. If May would only help her slip out of this world and into the next, perhaps she could be with him again. At the very least, she'd no longer be tormented by his absence. Seven decades of suffering was enough.

Minty knew that she was a coward for insisting on May's help. Why didn't she just sort herself out? But there was a part of her, some awful, punishing part of herself, that refused to let go.

God knew she'd had opportunities. *La belle vie* had provided access to every pill and potion possible to make one feel wonderful, though too much was guaranteed to make one feel nothing at all. Forever after.

She could've jumped from a bridge, wearing something diaphanous that caught the air just right as she fell. Or driven off a cliff in Eduardo's red convertible, her once abundant hair streaming out behind her. Or just finished herself off by holding Mateo's ugly gun to her head, but that would've been a messy, horrible way to go.

Was Mateo the one with the gun or was that Phillippe? Or Zaid? No, it was definitely Mateo. He had the villa in Naples and that odd little pet monkey named Benito. Phillippe had the tiny flat in the Marais in the attic of an old mansion. The marble staircase leading up to his flat had been so cold on Minty's bare bottom. She smiled at the memory.

Yes, Mateo had the gun. He kept it in a drawer beside his bed for protection against intruders. It would have been so easy for Minty to have helped herself to it one night when Mateo was away doing whatever it was he did for a living.

But an open casket was almost certainly not a possibility

after a death like that. Minty definitely wanted an open casket so that her many admirers could look upon her one last time.

So many opportunities to end it, yet she'd never had the courage to do it. Then she'd remembered her secret weapon.

May had always been the one to get things done. Even as a child, May was the one who dealt with the difficult, boring parts of life. She'd kept the house running while sorting out her own education, as Minty downed martinis in the sitting room and Bertie snorted and raged, piling up more and more money.

May was the only one who'd ever stood up to her father. Poor, bitter Bertie. Not allowed to fight in the war because of his gammy leg. Deemed 'medically unfit'. How he hated that term. Minty would save it up and use it when she most wanted to hurt him. If he couldn't prove his manliness on the battlefield, then he would grow rich off the backs of the poor soldiers who could. Like her darling.

She held the locket against her chest, close to her heart.

One thing Minty had learned from almost a century of living was that life was lived in patterns. People couldn't help themselves. An ex-lover, who'd been her psychiatrist for a time, told Minty that we constantly repeat traumatic stories from childhood, trying to create a different ending. That new ending almost never happened, so we just end up stuck, repeating the same stories over and over again.

If I can just lose the weight/get the promotion/buy the sports car, I'll be happy at last.

If I'm good enough, I can make her love me.

He'll change for me and we'll be happy together.

It's all part of the human condition. Sometimes the pattern is repeated throughout a life, sometimes over generations. The stories, even the unhappy ones, become comforting with familiarity, trapping us in an endless loop. With careful thought and observation, the patterns can be revealed, though changing them takes an enormous amount of willpower and frequently a great deal of pain. Often, when one has tried one's hardest to push back against these relentless forces, the story one was fighting against will still be repeated, just with a slightly different twist.

Like May, trying so hard to avoid men like her father, then marrying someone who, deep down, was cut from exactly the same cloth. Instead of bellowing and barbarism, things one can see and recognise and avoid, James Faraday weaponised kindness and piety. His form of bullying was invisible to the outside world, where he flattered and charmed, as he slowly and meticulously sucked the life out of May with his little comments and criticisms. Carefully, he chipped away at May's spirit and independence. Minty had watched her vibrant, demanding child become fretful and self-conscious. Always trying to please the beloved James. It had been too painful to bear.

Then the bastard had left May for another woman. How Minty would love to get her hands on James Faraday. Preferably wrapped tightly round his flabby neck.

But Minty's lovely, difficult child was returning. Fletcher was bringing her back. For this, Minty was grateful. It was the tempestuous, volatile version of May who would finally help her find peace.

The voices in the kitchen had gone quiet. What were they up to now?

Minty scooted out of the armchair and went to investigate. The kitchen was empty, no May or Fletcher to be seen, but voices could be heard outside in the little courtyard. She attempted to silently slide open the window beside the table to listen. The old sash scraped and whined. The voices immediately stopped.

Minty pushed the window all the way open with a bang and stuck her head out. The courtyard was deserted but she spotted the toes of two pairs of shoes, one set of suede brogues and another of tan flats, poking from behind a brick pilaster. The sound of giggling and a puff of smoke appeared from behind it. Minty pulled her head back inside, smiling to herself.

She closed the window and turned to the dogs on their bed beside the Aga. 'Some things never change,' she said. 'Still hiding from me for a smoke.' She shook her head as she walked out of the kitchen. 'At least it's not those dreadful skunky-smelling things they used to smoke when they'd come home from Cambridge.'

CHAPTER THREE

HOW SWEET IT IS (TO BE LOVED BY YOU)

Fletcher was ensconced in his study with the door locked. He'd popped into the village and purchased padlocks for both his and Barb's wardrobes in an attempt to keep Minty out. He just hoped she didn't have May's knack for picking locks.

He looked down at his phone.

> Some rise by sin. I know all about the unnatural acts you commit with your manservant. DP

May had forwarded him the strange text, saying almost everyone in the bookshop had received it. Odd.

The only person he knew in Blackheath with a manservant was the vicar of St Julian's, the church on the heath. Father David and his partner, Juan, had been together for years but, to maintain a sense of propriety, Juan was technically employed as a housekeeper and general myrmidon.

DP?

Was that referring to Father David Panagos or were they the initials of the sender?

Unnatural acts?

He supposed that depended on one's point of view. As far as Fletcher knew, David wasn't into anything that might frighten the horses. But *et vivere, reservate*, what one got up to within the privacy of one's own bedroom was no one else's business.

Fletcher's thoughts naturally turned to Sparks, his current *amatus*. Dear, warm, sweet Sparks. They were meeting later to make dinner using the early asparagus from Sparks's garden. Fletcher had spent the afternoon baking a fresh loaf of sourdough to dip into the soup.

Gerald Chanda, better known as Sparks, was the whole package. A handsome, funny man who really knew his way around a kohlrabi. Fletcher felt a little shiver of anticipation.

Who would be having dinner with Sparks tonight? Fletcher or his alter ego, Barb?

Lately, it seemed that Barb only came out to write her books or, every once in a while, she'd be part of a social occasion. May had hosted several drinks evenings over the last few months and Barb loved an opportunity to dress up.

But Barb could sometimes feel like a lot of work. The hair, the make-up, the choosing of the outfit, the confining shoes. More often than not, Fletcher just wanted to be comfortable.

He looked down at his current ensemble. He was wearing a pair of what they used to call Oxford bags, wide-legged trousers built for comfort and dancing, a dress shirt open at the collar and a cashmere waistcoat in a shade of blue that exactly matched his eyes. His grey tweed and a splash of Floris No. 89 would be enough. No need to get out the lipstick and curling tongs. Sparks would be delighted to see him, whatever he was wearing.

Decision made, his eyes returned to the text message. Unpleasant. Fletcher had experienced more than his fair share of nastiness over the years. Perhaps he would just check in with David and Juan.

———

That evening, in Sparks's cosy flat, replete with hot soup and fresh bread, the two men relaxed on the squishy sofa. Fletcher rested his feet in Sparks's lap and told him about the text message.

'Do you think it was referring to David?' Sparks asked, rubbing a foot with one hand while sipping from his glass of cognac with the other.

Fletcher shrugged. 'I don't know who else it could be. That sign-off, DP. It seems too much of a coincidence to think it doesn't refer to David and Juan.' He swirled the golden liquid in his glass. 'I suppose it might be nothing, but it does sound rather sinister.' He sighed. 'David was unfazed when I spoke to him. Juan's a bit under the weather but wasn't concerned about the message either. I'm sure they've heard it all before.'

'Could just be teenagers playing silly buggers,' Sparks said. He was a semi-retired computer science teacher at the local comprehensive and was no longer shocked by anything that young people did. 'Doesn't sound like kids though. They'd go straight for something obvious like "bumfuck" or "arse bandit". "Unnatural acts" is positively subtle.'

'Some people have too much time on their hands,' Fletcher said, sipping his drink.

Sparks's hand moved inside the wide trouser leg to massage Fletcher's calf. 'Are you sure you won't come to the coast with me tomorrow?' Sparks had inherited a family house near Goldhanger on the River Blackwater.

Fletcher shook his head. 'Not this time. I think May needs

me around. Minty is reaching fever pitch.' He chuckled. 'You know, I rather like "arse bandit". I'm picturing you in a mask and striped shirt. You'd look quite dashing.'

Sparks scooted closer on the sofa, moving his hand up Fletcher's thigh. 'That, my sweet, can be arranged.'

CHAPTER FOUR

WHERE DID OUR LOVE GO?

The following morning May lay in bed staring at the wall and feeling melancholy. Fletcher had stayed at Sparks's place, leaving her to have dinner alone with her mother. She didn't begrudge Fletcher his romance, May would've done the same given half a chance, but she was struggling with a deep encroaching loneliness. James had been gone for almost a year and a half. Devastation had occupied the first few months of his absence, then the logistics of adjusting to her new normal had taken time. Fletcher had kept her busy and distracted. They'd even had a little adventure searching for a missing girl. It was almost like old times. She'd learned to embrace the euphoria of her new-found independence.

Then Minty arrived and Fletcher had begun spending more time with Sparks. May found herself at a loose end. She'd given up volunteering at the church, floated from one activity to another: Zumba (horrid), taxidermy (fascinating, but smelly), *krav maga* (much more useful, then her instructor married and immigrated to Australia). The Italian class had been a bore. The fencing class was the same. It was all drab church halls full of drab people trying to find a way to pass the time until death released them from their drab lives. If distraction was all May wanted, she could've passed the time at home in her own library.

She'd been hanging around the bookshop more often until she realised she was getting in Bastian's way. May might own the shop, but it was firmly Bastian's domain. He was the bookshop's *compère*, the master of ceremonies and chairman of the shop's social network.

She gave a deep, shuddering sigh from the depths of the duvet, trying to pull herself together enough to get out of bed and begin the day. May was grieving, not just for the end of her marriage but for a lost future too. James's departure meant that her whole world had shifted, from the weekly grocery shop (no more kippers or yoghurt fruit corners) to how she viewed herself in the world, no longer part of a couple. In the years he was fighting cancer, she'd prepared herself for his death. At times it felt imminent, but he'd always pulled through. Somehow, his leaving felt worse. If he'd died, she would've been able to grieve and move on. As it stood, he was still alive, still out there somewhere, happier than he'd been with her. She dreaded turning a corner and bumping into him, witnessing his happiness while she was still struggling. Or, even worse, having him barge back into her life in some way.

May had recently realised that some part of her had thought, even hoped, that James would return. That being away from her would make him realise his mistake and he'd come back, sheepish and apologetic. Then their life, their plans for a future together, would resume. It was humiliating to admit such a thing, even only to herself. Did she even want him back? The time apart had allowed her to see her husband of forty years in a different light. He did not come off well in the analysis.

Distance had provided clarity and she'd realised the many times he'd been uncaring and cold, contributing the bare minimum to their relationship. May had come to feel invisible in her own home. James had a way of making it seem that May was always the one at fault. That she was overly sensitive, too demanding, hysterical even. Yet, in public he was always courteous and attentive, obsequious even. It was a complete mindfuck.

She had come to realise that she definitely did not want him back, but adjusting to this new normal would take time. The process was just taking much longer than she liked. There were obviously still many cumbersome emotions to process and Minty's presence wasn't helping.

Having her mother in the house reminded May too much of a childhood spent with unhappy parents. The ghosts of all those old feelings of discontent were colluding with her current sense of sadness to create a monster of melancholia.

When he was home, her irritable, sulking father would be in his office shouting at someone on the telephone, while Minty drank herself into a stupor in her sitting room. Little May had adored her funny, glamorous mother, but Minty was often too wrapped up in her own problems to have time for the children. She'd sit alone, clutching her locket and staring off into space.

Little May had often wondered what was in the locket. More than once, she'd walked in on Minty crying while looking at it, or even talking to it. When she saw May watching her, Minty would close the locket with a snap and shoo May out of the room.

May had been appalled to see that her mother still kept a portrait of her younger self beside her bed. Who does that? May couldn't imagine doing such a thing. She tried to remember if there were any photos of herself displayed in Greenway and realised that her wedding portrait was the only one.

That was a reason to get up. She'd take down that photo and put it away where she wouldn't have to look at it anymore. May decided if removing that photo was the only thing she accomplished all day, it would be enough.

Throwing back the duvet, she remained lying in bed, unable to make herself sit up. Could she pretend to be ill and just stay in bed all day? She tried to unpick the threads of her gloom, to organise her emotions, directing them to their proper sources, but she felt so tired. Sometimes it was easier to just feel the sadness, let it wash over her until the moment passed and she was free to get on with her life.

The dogs. The dogs needed her. Since Fletcher was away, she would be the one to feed them and let them out. It would never have crossed Minty's mind to do such a thing.

May would get out of bed for Bess and George.

In the kitchen, hair still in sleepy tufts, she prepared the moka pot and placed it on the hob, then fed Bess and George, giving them each a fresh bone for a treat. Blackheath Village had a new butcher, Nick, who was charm personified and generous with his leftovers.

Once the coffee was ready, she sat at the big pine table that had been in Greenway's kitchen for generations. The room had changed very little since May's childhood. The sunny yellow cabinets and terrazzo countertops had been chosen by Minty when she was a young wife and mother. May could remember with absolute clarity what it felt like to bump her head on the corner of that countertop and how precarious it felt to stand with her feet balanced on that shelf as she watched Minty preparing a meal. The edge of the shelf still bore the damage from young May's Mary Janes.

Minty had been a surprisingly good cook, a skill which had not passed from mother to daughter. Perhaps May would sign up for a cooking class?

No. She made a face. The idea held no interest. Besides, Fletcher was an excellent cook. Too many chefs and all that. Surely, she could think of better ways to spend her time.

'Good morning.' Minty bustled into the kitchen. 'Oof, you look like the dog's dinner this morning. Bad night?' she said, as she filled and switched on the kettle.

'Thanks for that,' May said. 'How long have you been up?' Minty seemed to barely sleep at all at night. She did most of her dozing during the day.

'I've been up for ages. Went for a walk and bumped into that nice Humphrey Oslac. Remember him? Mildred Oslac's boy.' She prepared a tray with the good Blue Willow teapot, cups, and saucers.

'I wouldn't describe Humphrey Oslac as a boy,' May said, thinking of the retired bus driver who lived on the other side of the village. He was the son of her old drama teacher at Blackheath High.

'You had such a crush on him.' Minty laughed. 'He barely noticed you, but you'd follow him around the village like a little lost dog.'

'Hmmm, recollections may vary,' May replied. She sipped her coffee, thinking of the handsome young man with grabby hands who revelled in the attention when he'd visited his mother at the all-girls school.

'I saw that odd man from next door. He was wearing what looked like a bullet-proof vest while exercising on the heath.' Minty poured boiling water into the teapot.

'I think it's a weighted vest,' May replied. 'Geoffrey seems to be on some kind of health kick.'

'He kept talking about his glucose levels and insisting I should have a faecal analysis, of all things. He even offered to submit my specimen for me as he seems to have a connection to some lab where he gives his own regular samples. Honestly.'

Minty shook her head in bewilderment. 'Is this a new fetish? I've never heard of such a thing.'

May rolled her eyes. 'Did you not get the whole lecture on the gut microbiome? He calls it our "second brain". I think, in Geoffrey's case, his bowels may constitute his only brain. I assume the term is taken straight from some ad he's seen. Geoffrey is very impressionable.' May sipped her tea. 'I think you should do it. Why don't you drop a sample round to Geoffrey's this afternoon?'

Minty tilted her head, seeming to think it over. 'How does one prepare such a thing? Tupperware? Coffee mug? Sandwich bag? Perhaps a nondescript paper bag?'

'Set aflame on his front porch?' May said.

'I believe that's referred to as a Hot Brown Betty,' Minty replied.

May laughed in spite of herself.

There was a knock at the front door.

'Speaking of Bettys,' Minty said, nodding towards the sound. She picked up the tray carefully and turned to leave with a twinkle in her eye. 'Humphrey sends his best, by the way.' If May didn't know better, she'd think Minty was trying to play matchmaker.

When Minty had made it clear that she'd come home to stay, May had asked Betty Danvers for help. Though Minty was in fine fettle for a woman of her age, there were challenges to be managed. Pills to remember, creams to apply, assistance with certain ablutions. May and Minty did not have the kind of relationship that allowed such intimacies. A nurse was needed.

Betty was delighted to assist. Her mother had passed away the previous winter and then, on their first holiday away in years, her husband Chester had died from a heart attack. It must've been a very difficult Christmas, but Betty proved to be remarkably resilient, throwing herself into organising the church volunteers and doing care work where needed.

Betty seemed to be handling her new solo life well. Perhaps May could learn a thing or two from her.

May listened as Minty opened the front door, heard Betty's hello and their morning greetings before another voice joined them.

'Coo-ee!' the voice said. 'It's only me!'

May slumped in her chair. It was Jilly's day to clean.

Jilly Bellamy had been cleaning for May for years. Friendly and boisterous, Jilly had probably played a lot of hockey at school. She'd been a teacher at St Julian's Primary School until she realised that she truly detested children. She said the cleaning job gave her more flexibility, more money, and kept her fit in the process.

May grumbled to herself. Though she liked Jilly and was very pleased to have her home cleaned by such a capable person, it was always rather annoying having someone coming and going through literally every space in the house all morning. May and the dogs would scuttle from room to room, trying their best to avoid the roar of the hoover and the all-encompassing pine-scented mist from Jilly's spray bottle.

Perhaps May would take the dogs to the coast for the day. Walking along the shingle at Dungeness would clear her head and improve her mood.

The hoover roared into life in the entry hall as the dogs came clamouring into the kitchen. May made up her mind.

She bent forward to scratch their floppy ears. George raised her silvery head, enjoying the attention until Bess pushed in, jealous as always. 'There's enough love for both of you,' May said. 'I'll throw some clothes on and we'll get out of this madhouse. What do you say to that?'

Then she picked up her phone, read the message on the screen and everything changed.

CHAPTER FIVE

BEER BARREL POLKA

B etty Danvers was the type of person Minty usually hated. May had told her that Betty, always immaculate, had a home that was tastefully and beautifully decorated without a single scuff on the stairs or squashed cushion on the sofa. She'd married her school sweetheart, and they had one daughter, a doctor who travelled the world with *Médecins Sans Frontières*. Originally a nurse, Betty had left work to care for her mother who'd always suffered with poor health. An active member of the WI, Betty turned out award-winning jams, chutneys and pickles every year. Her Christmas mincemeat was a village favourite. She knitted. She quilted. She read to the children at St Julian's Primary School. She volunteered at the church. By all accounts Betty Danvers was an absolute saint. It was perfectly disgusting.

Minty would've truly detested Betty if she hadn't been such a genuinely warm and caring person. In private, Betty also liked to dish the dirt on everyone in the village, which helped. Too much goodness was always suspect.

On her arrival at Greenway in January, Minty had taken over the front sitting room. May came home one afternoon to find builders adapting the downstairs shower room and moving May's furniture to the attic. In its place was Minty's enormous four-poster bed, with little steps leading up to the high mattress. A framed portrait of a young Minty sat on the bedside table, taken by her darling boy on their final day together. Her trunks were arranged along one wall beside a new vanity unit with an upholstered stool, where Minty could arrange her hair and put on her face each morning. She'd kept two armchairs by the window where she could sit, methodically judging passers-by.

It was in these chairs that Minty and Betty were convening, sipping cups of Earl Grey, when May came in looking for Fletcher.

'Has he come back from Sparks's yet?' May asked, looking unusually flustered, still in her dressing gown. The hoover hummed in another room downstairs.

'I've no idea,' Minty said. 'Has something happened?'

'Perhaps,' May mumbled as she left the room.

Minty looked at Betty. 'I wonder what that was about.'

Betty shrugged. 'Tell me more about the dances in the caves.' She sipped her tea and settled her bony bottom more deeply into the armchair.

Minty smiled. It was unusual for anyone to take such an interest in her old stories. The last time she'd seen Betty, Minty had told her about the Blackheath caves, created by chalk miners in the seventeenth century, or perhaps even long before then. They'd been sealed up for years until Minty and her friends had rediscovered them.

'We weren't supposed to be there at all. Jacquie and John Cady found an entrance to the caves in their garden when a sinkhole appeared one summer. Life was still hard after the war with rationing and rebuilding still going on. It was wonderful to have a secret place where we could escape from our worries for a bit, pretend all that doom and gloom couldn't touch us.'

'Wasn't it dangerous?' Betty asked.

'Probably.' Minty shrugged. 'But we were all still young and immortal. We'd survived a war with bombs dropping around us every night. Many of our friends and loved ones had gone to fight and never returned. The ones who did make it back weren't the same when they came home. Even if their bodies were undamaged, their minds were a different story.' She sighed. 'A hole in the ground held no fear for us. We'd put on our glad rags, any old thing with a bit of sparkle, then shimmy down that muddy hole and have the time of our lives.'

Just like May, Minty had been born at Greenway and grown up in Blackheath. She was familiar with all the old families and most of their secrets. The Morrigans had been a part of Blackheath for generations. Greenway had been in the family since 1730, passed down through the years. Minty's great grandfather had been a canny old git and included a clause in his will stating that only a Morrigan could ever own the house. If a female child was to inherit, she would need to maintain the name of Morrigan after marriage, as well as any issue from that union. When there were no Morrigans left, the house reverted to Greenwich Council to do with as they wished. The council was very much aware of this clause. The big Georgian building overlooking Blackheath was a landmark in the village, a prime piece of real estate. Therefore, the council kept a close eye on the comings and goings at Greenway.

Because Minty had detached from the world when she married Bertie, her memories of her youth in Blackheath were well-preserved, like a mosquito trapped in amber a million years ago. Every detail, every nuance remained clear in her recollections, only hardened and sharpened by time.

Minty could remember it all. The initial thrill of their discovery of the caves. The cool scent of the chalk walls of the caverns mixed with burning beeswax candles. The filthy chandelier they'd cleaned with a bucket of water, studded with candles and rehung from the ceiling of the largest cave. The old stone bar in the corner, littered with broken bottles, most of them over a century old. They'd collected the coloured glass, cleaned it and used it to decorate the walls of their sanctuary. The old glass sparkled like jewels in the candlelight.

That's where Minty met her darling.

'Your grandmother used to come to the parties,' she told Betty. 'She was younger than the rest of us, but your Great Aunt Elsie would bring her along sometimes.'

They'd been an odd pair. Vibrant, gutsy Elsie and the precocious, haughty little Lizzie. She acted like butter wouldn't melt but, deep down, the girl was as cold-blooded as a snake. Odd that this nice woman was her granddaughter.

'There was a big cave and two smaller ones,' Minty said. 'One of the smaller caves had a deep well in it, so we stayed out of there in case anyone tumbled in. The other one we called the Good Time Grotto because... well, you can imagine. There were still a lot of khaki-wackies about. You know, women who were overly fond of a man in uniform.' She tutted.

Minty had not been one of the wackies. Years spent watching her mother cater to her father's every whim had soured Minty to the idea of love and marriage. As soon as she was old enough, and much to her parents' distress, she'd found herself a job selling hats at Liberty & Co. When war broke out, Minty became a conductress on the 47 bus running from Bellingham to Shoreditch. She'd loved working on the buses, writing the tickets and going round with her punch to check them. After the war, when the men returned, she'd been heartbroken to be relegated back to selling pretty things again.

Her parents had done their best to marry her off to any eligible bachelor in the village, but Minty always resisted. She had her fun, but no one was going to tie her down. Until he caught her eye. At first, she thought he was nothing but a ladies' man. There for a good time, but nothing more. Then they'd spent the night together in the caves.

When the others had left, they'd lingered, talking and laughing. They ended up stretched out, head-to-head, along the length of the long bar, feet pointing in opposite directions, Minty wrapped in his wool greatcoat. There they lay, with only the tops of their heads touching, chatting until the candles burned down, leaving only their voices to rise into the darkness, weaving their stories together. When the sun rose, casting a dim light into the cave, Minty realised that she was very much in love.

It wasn't the uniform that had attracted her. It was the strange feeling of coming home that had settled in her bones the moment she sat up and looked into his eyes.

'What was Gran like?' Betty asked, breaking into Minty's gentle memories. Betty then leaned forward and said in a lower tone, 'You didn't hear it from me, but Aunt Elsie was always the black sheep of the family. I'm sure she spent plenty of time in the Good Time Grotto.' She made a disapproving face.

Minty had fond memories of Elsie. Like herself, she'd avoided marriage and had a job. While Minty worked at the shop in town, Elsie had worked in a café in Lewisham. Both of them were in their twenties and had a sense of freedom and autonomy that many of their married contemporaries did not. Minty couldn't remember Elsie spending any time in the Good Time Grotto. In fact, Minty reflected now, Elsie's tastes ran more to the feminine. It was her little sister, Betty's grandmother, who was known as Loose Legs Lizzie.

'I always liked Elsie,' Minty said. 'She had a good head on her shoulders.' Elsie had eventually bought out the owners of the Bluebird Café, which was still popular in Lewisham. May and Fletcher had taken Minty there for tea and cake a few times. She'd been pleased to see another spirited young woman working behind the counter.

'What about Gran? I don't expect she was much fun,' Betty said.

True, unless you were male.

'She was a wonderful dancer,' Minty said diplomatically.

'Gran?! Lizzie Miller? Are you sure you're thinking of the right person?' Betty sat forward in her chair, delighted with the information.

'Oh yes, Lizzie did a lovely foxtrot. She and Ed were by far the best dancers in the group.' Minty remembered Lizzie, all of sixteen, swirling and being thrown through the air by the dashing Ed. He was always in demand. Loose Legs Lizzie had to fight off many other admirers to be by his side.

Betty laughed and clapped her hands. 'I had no idea. I wonder if Mum knew.' She looked wistful. 'I'm named Elizabeth after Gran, but I can't dance for toffee,' she said. 'I never knew my granddad. He died when Mum was little. Do you remember that?'

'Yes, it was such a shock. He was still so young.' Ed's drinking had soon got out of hand after Lizzie fell pregnant and they had to marry. It was a bad match for both of them.

He'd been found by the milkman one morning, face down in Blackheath Pond beside the Princess of Wales pub with a big dent in the back of his head. Rumour had it that Lizzie had finally had enough of his drinking and carousing, though nothing could ever be proven.

Poor Ed.

'Mum says he had a massive heart attack. There was nothing anyone could do to save him.'

How interesting.

Minty looked at Betty's face, which seemed to be in earnest. Fascinating, the secrets families kept from one another. Who had started the lie? Loose Legs Lizzie or Betty's mother? Minty's money was on Lizzie. 'Hmmm,' Minty said, feigning forgetfulness. 'I don't remember all the details. It was all such a long time ago. Something smells lovely.' She nodded towards the basket beside Betty's chair. 'Have you been baking again?'

Betty blushed. 'Yes, I brought you some more hot cross buns. I'm still using up the Christmas mincemeat. I seem to have a lot left over this year.'

'They smell divine,' Minty said. 'Shall we have some now?'

'I'm sick of the sight of them, but you tuck in,' Betty said as she pulled the little wicker basket closer.

CHAPTER SIX

I HEARD IT THROUGH THE GRAPEVINE

Fletcher stretched luxuriously in Sparks's enormous bed. The sun was bright round the edges of the curtains. He'd slept later than usual. Having Minty in the house had been taking a toll on Fletcher's sleep. The constant tension and bickering, Minty's music at all hours of the night, made it difficult to relax.

Sparks entered the bedroom carrying a tray laid with a cafetière, mugs and slices of hot, buttered toast. He was still sleepily scruffy in a pair of flannel pyjama bottoms with his hair standing on end. Fletcher's heart melted at the sight of him.

'Good morning, my love,' Sparks said.

'You're an absolute angel,' Fletcher replied, sitting up and making room for the tray on the bed. He stretched again, adding a yawn for good measure.

Sparks opened the curtains and cracked the window open, filling the room with sunlight and fresh air. 'How did you sleep?' he asked.

'Like the dead,' Fletcher said. It was so peaceful at Sparks's flat. The large Victorian house was divided into six flats, all owned by couples or individuals. No children, no pets, no Lou

Preager at 4am. He patted the bed for Sparks to join him, bit into some toast and picked up his phone from the bedside table.

Fletcher sat up suddenly, disturbing the peace and almost upsetting the coffee tray. 'I've got to go home,' he said. 'Right now.'

Crossing the heath towards Greenway, Fletcher wondered what could possibly have happened.

> Juan is dead

May's message was unequivocal, but how? David had said that Juan wasn't feeling well the night before but hadn't seemed unduly concerned. Just a stomach bug. How had a stomach bug escalated so quickly? Or was there more to it?

Fletcher sent a quick text to David, to see if there was anything he could do.

'Dr Redmond?' A young woman was standing on the heath in front of Greenway. She held out her phone as Fletcher approached. 'Dr Fletcher Redmond?' she said.

'Yes,' Fletcher replied. He didn't recognise her from the village.

'Is it true you've been living a double life as the romance novelist Barbara Bouvier for decades?' She tilted the phone towards Fletcher, and he realised she was filming him.

Fletcher stopped in his tracks. 'I beg your pardon,' he said. 'Who are you?'

'My name is Marcia Jackson. I'm with the *National Observer*. Could you please answer the question, Dr Redmond.' She thrust the phone forward.

Fletcher recoiled. 'I have no idea what you're talking about,' he said. 'Now, if you'll excuse me. I'm trying to get home.'

To her credit, Marcia Jackson stepped aside. 'I'll speak to you soon, Dr Redmond,' she said as Fletcher passed, heading for Greenway's front porch.

Once inside, he leaned against the door, head spinning. 'What the fuck was that all about?' he mumbled. But it was not the time to worry about rude journalists, he needed to find May and learn more about Juan's death.

'Is that you, Fletcher?' May opened the doors to her library and motioned him inside. He dropped into an armchair beside the fireplace.

'Has the world gone mad?' he asked, as the dogs jumped into his lap. He looked at May properly. 'You're not dressed.'

May looked down at her dressing gown. 'That is correct,' she said. 'Well observed, Watson.'

She closed the doors behind her then came to sit across from Fletcher. 'You got my text?'

Fletcher nodded. 'Why do you think I've come rushing back? What's happened? How did you find out?' He settled the dogs on his lap where they immediately started to doze.

'I've only heard it from Darcy so far, but she's very reliable,' May said. Darcy Cooper knew everyone and everything that happened in Blackheath Village. Her all-seeing eyes were made gigantic by the thick glasses she wore. Her hair was an unruly tangle of curls, usually standing on end. May presumed the curls were aerials in disguise, tapping into radio frequencies only Darcy could hear.

'Darcy says that Juan took ill yesterday, upset stomach and feeling rough. He went to bed early then woke in the night struggling to breathe. David thought he was having a stroke, Juan could barely speak, so he rang for an ambulance and Juan was rushed to hospital. They did what they could, but he died early this morning.'

'How awful,' Fletcher said. 'David must be devastated. They've been together for years.' His thoughts turned to Sparks. They'd only known each other a relatively short time, but it was already agony to consider life without him. 'Juan seems fairly young for a stroke. How old was he? Fifty? Fifty-five?'

'That's the thing, Fletch,' May said. 'It wasn't a stroke. Juan was poisoned.'

CHAPTER SEVEN

I CAN'T HELP MYSELF (SUGAR PIE, HONEY BUNCH)

'Poisoned?!'

May was gratified to see Fletcher sit upright in his armchair at this information, causing the dogs to grumble.

'Yes,' she said. 'Arsenic, they think.'

'Arsenic? How on earth did Juan swallow *arsenic*?' he replied, settling back for the sake of the dogs. Bess and George re-staked their claims by burrowing deeper. 'I can't imagine how that could happen.'

'Well, exactly,' May said. 'That's the question.'

'Is David all right?' Fletcher asked. 'He wasn't exposed to it as well?'

'No.' She shook her head. 'I haven't heard that he was ill. Just Juan. Poor David must be in an absolute state though.'

They sat in silence for a moment. Each in their own world of reflection as the hoover thumped back and forth upstairs.

One couldn't exactly buy arsenic at the local Sainsbury's. Not like in the past when it was used in everything from dyes to pesticides to beauty therapies.

May had already started conducting her research on the subject. Her desk in the library was strewn with books with The

Pharmaceutical Society's *Guide to Poisons* front and centre. Since her days working at the British Library, she'd found information comforting. May had read that most modern-day arsenic poisoning came from long-term exposure to contaminated water. But in that case, Juan would've experienced other symptoms, like a sore throat and lesions on his hands. Things that wouldn't be ignored. Things that would've made him go to the doctor and get help.

No, he must've ingested a large dose all at once.

May had once looked into how she might produce arsenic for her own uses. The complicated process required had put her off. Too much of a faff when there were so many more potent poisons which were much easier to extract and condense.

Arsenic was an interesting choice if the poisoning had been intentional. The strange text message she'd received the day before the death meant that it almost certainly had to be.

'Are you thinking about the text?' Fletcher asked.

'Yes,' May replied. 'It feels like it must be connected. Too much of a coincidence for a message like that to be sent the morning before Juan's death. Unless he was so distraught by the text that he decided to kill himself?' That didn't sound like Juan. He'd always seemed particularly resilient, a constant support to David and his work in the parish. But May knew that one never really knew what was going on inside another person's head. 'Why don't we go see David. I'm sure he can use some support right now.'

After they both freshened up, May deposited the dogs with Minty in her room, then they set off across the heath towards the vicarage.

The church, St Julian's, sat proudly on the southern edge of the heath, surrounded by the green on all sides. Though its stained glass had been lost in the Blitz, the Kentish ragstone exterior seemed to glow in the spring sunshine, the tall spire pointing at the cloudless blue sky as if to say 'How can anyone deny the presence of God when such beauty exists'.

May and Fletcher stopped at the church to peek into the empty nave and vestry, thinking that David might be seeking solace there. They found only Mordecai Page, the building's caretaker, muttering to himself as he swept fallen blossom from the porch.

Mordecai was a string bean of a man with a greasy combover and chronic halitosis.

'Have you seen Father David?' May asked.

Mordecai stopped, leaned on his broom, and sighed. Almost the same age as Minty, Mordecai Page had earned the right to his cantankerous attitude by lying about his age in order to fight in World War II, then being captured and held as a prisoner of war for years, though May secretly suspected he'd been a grumpy old coot from birth. Mordecai scowled, scratched his nether regions, then spat, causing Fletcher to jump out of the splatter zone. 'Nah,' he said at last. He returned to his sweeping.

'Right,' May replied. Accustomed to the ways of Mordecai Page, she waited with arms crossed while Fletcher wiped his shoes with a hanky.

Mordecai moved the broom back and forth, stirring the blossom about rather than removing it, while glaring at May the whole time, but no one could beat May Morrigan when it came to a stare-off. Eventually Mordecai broke. ''E was 'ere afore, crying 'is eyes out o'er the death of 'is butler. Disgusting it is,' he mumbled. 'A'right for some with their servants 'n maids 'n all. Not like us what cleans up their messes.' He spat again, but even Mordecai Page knew better than to spit anywhere near May Morrigan's shoes. 'Said 'e was going 'ome.'

'Thank you, Mordecai,' May said as she and Fletcher turned back towards the village and the new vicarage on the other side. The original vicarage, a grand Victorian building overlooking

Blackheath, had been sold off to raise funds for essential repairs to the church after WWII. It had been divided into flats then sold off bit by bit, tripling the purchase price. The 'new' vicarage was a Span house, purpose-built in the 1950s. A boxy, modular home that had been radical at the time, it was, to May's eyes, a depressing piece of architecture.

David answered their knock which was, in itself, unsettling. Juan had always been the one to open the door, answer the vicarage phone, provide refreshments for visitors. David would certainly be lost without him. He looked exhausted, his face puffy and eyes pink from weeping.

May and Fletcher followed him into the kitchen then sat him down at the small table near the wall of windows at the back. The beautiful day and luscious green garden (another of Juan's many talents) were in stark contrast to David's sombre expression. 'He's going to miss the dahlias,' he said, voice wavering. 'Juan loved the dahlias most of all the flowers.'

May pulled the vertical blinds shut with a snap then went to wash her hands at the kitchen sink. Just speaking to Mordecai Page had left her feeling unclean.

'We've just come from the church,' she said. 'Mordecai told us you'd come home. The man is a nuisance, David. You really should retire him. He's not even good at his job.'

Father David nodded. 'The volunteers were complaining about him. Apparently, he hides pornography in the crypt utility cupboard.' He tried to smile, but it came out as a grimace. 'Men like Mordecai are unhappy creatures. I pity the man.'

'You're too good, David,' May replied. 'I guess that's why you're a vicar and I'm not.'

Fletcher had been opening cupboards, preparing drinks for them. 'How do you operate this thing?' he asked, turning the Nespresso coffee maker this way and that.

'Don't touch that!' David shouted. He stood beside the

table, his thinning hair forming a messy quiff. 'Only Juan uses the Nespresso. He loves... *loved* the damn thing.' He collapsed back onto the chair with his head in his hands. 'Leave the machine and its blasted pods. I never drink coffee. The teabags are in the cupboard.' He gestured limply then put his head down on the table. 'I apologise for shouting. I just can't bear to think of anyone touching his things.'

'Did Juan use the machine yesterday morning?' May asked.

David nodded, bumping his forehead against the table.

'But you didn't?' she said.

'No, I just said that, didn't I.' David raised his head and scowled at them, then started weeping again. 'I'm sorry,' he said, laying his head back down on the table.

May exchanged a look with Fletcher. 'That's perfectly understandable,' she said. 'Come, David. Let's get comfortable and Fletcher can bring us all a nice hot cup of tea.' She helped David out of the dining chair, leaving a small pool of tears behind on the tabletop. They crossed the tiny hallway to the sitting room where she plopped him onto an armchair. He sat staring into oblivion, back hunched, chin resting on his chest, like an old turtle without its shell.

May perched on an armchair that was firmer than it looked, and inspected the boxy white room. It was a meagre space, lacking in both square footage and charm, but David and Juan had made it into a home. One wall was lined with bookshelves. She spotted Tom Wright's hefty biography of St Paul next to Ottolenghi's *Jerusalem* cookbook. There were framed photos of David and Juan taken on their travels. May recognised the Wailing Wall in one, a jokey snap of Juan holding up the Leaning Tower of Pisa in another. There was a photo of them taken on some beach, laughing towards the camera, faces pressed together, glasses held high. The love and joy shared by the two men was so evident. Her mind wandered to the staid photos taken of her and James over the years, always at least a foot of space between them as they posed in front of some monument or landmark. May's heart contracted in her chest. She was horrified to realise that she was about to cry.

Fletcher came in with the tea and the moment thankfully passed. May took all of those messy, difficult emotions and pushed them back down where they belonged.

'Here we are,' Fletcher said, sitting a tray down on the coffee table. 'Now, tell us all about it.'

David took the mug of tea Fletcher offered him, holding it carefully without taking a sip. He took in a lungful of air, as if preparing to dive into deep water. 'Juan started feeling poorly yesterday afternoon,' he said. 'We thought it was just a stomach bug, so I made him a glass of Andrews Salts and he took himself to bed. He was up and down in the night, poor thing, and feeling dreadful. Then, suddenly, it was like he couldn't breathe. He was gasping for air, could barely speak. That's when I rang for the ambulance.'

David looked towards the window where a vibrant rose bush was in full bloom. He closed his eyes. 'And then, he died.'

'I'm so sorry, David,' Fletcher said, moving to sit beside the vicar on the sofa.

'I think we need more milk,' May said, standing up and taking the small jug from the tray with her. She left Fletcher to console David while she had a quick snoop around.

In the kitchen, she found the bin under the sink and carefully sifted through the layers of rubbish. A bread bag, an empty tin of tomato soup, dirty paper towels, soggy teabags, greasy scrapings from a frying pan, eggshells... and then she found what she was searching for. Used coffee pods.

David had said that only Juan used the Nespresso machine. Could someone have poisoned the coffee pods? There were two of the little foil domes in the bin. May took one, leaving the other for the police, whom she hoped would eventually be asking the same questions.

The bread bag had avoided the greasy leavings and was reasonably clean. She removed it, shaking the crumbs into the bin before popping the coffee pod inside. She shifted the pod into a corner of the bag then tied it off, sealing it into its own small bubble.

Checking through the cupboards, she found the container of Andrews Salts and carefully spooned some of the powder into another corner of the bread bag before tying it off as well. It wasn't perfect, certainly not sterile, but it would do.

If someone had poisoned Juan through the coffee or the salts, May would soon find out.

CHAPTER EIGHT

WAIT

When they finally left the vicarage, Fletcher was shattered. He'd been wondering how they would ever be able to leave David to his grief. After telling his tale, the poor man had lapsed into a stolid silence, still gripping the cup of tea whilst staring at the roses. May and Fletcher had remained, trying to make small talk with David before giving up and chatting amongst themselves. Then Jilly had arrived, opening the door with her key, shouting 'Coo-ee!' into the subdued house.

She was clattering about with the mop and bucket from the hall cupboard when Fletcher told her what had happened. 'Blimey,' she said. 'I saw Mr Amador not two days ago and he was fit as a fiddle.'

Fletcher and May had left David in Jilly's capable hands. She was making sandwiches and running David a bath within minutes of hearing the sad news.

'I never got round to drinking my tea at David's,' Fletcher said, as they walked up the leafy street. 'Let's stop in the bookshop for a coffee. I'm not sure I can make it all the way home without some caffeine.'

'Good idea,' May replied. 'Grief is a remarkably unsparing emotion.'

'You were a long time fetching that milk,' he said, giving May a sideways glance as they made their way through the village. 'What were you up to?'

May turned innocent eyes on him. She looked so much like Minty when she did that. 'I don't know what you mean,' she said.

Fletcher smiled to himself, knowing very well that he would find out sooner or later.

The brass bell above the door jingled out its welcome when they entered the shop. Bastian raised his head and smiled in greeting. The smile disappeared when he saw their expressions.

'You've been to see David,' he said. 'Come on back, I've got a lovely Bakewell tart with your names on it.'

A few customers were browsing the stacks. Betty Danvers was looking through the section on Blackheath history and Geoffrey Crichton was poring over a keto cookbook. A mum and small child were sitting on the floor near the children's books, quietly reading to each other.

In the area at the rear of the shop Bastian had added an old chesterfield sofa, a couple of armchairs and a few tables and chairs. He hosted events and sold hot drinks and slices of cake in the cosy space.

Surprisingly few modifications had been needed to accommodate Bastian's height in May's bookshop. There were, perhaps, more stepladders than usual tucked beside the bookcases and small sets of steps behind the front counter and in the catering area. Bastian had chosen a high stool with a footrest to use behind the counter at the front of the shop when it was quiet. He could often be seen there, working on his laptop or reading. The book would usually be the latest non-fiction, though Fletcher had learned that the dust-cover didn't always match the book. More than once, he'd picked up some worthy-looking tome from the counter, only to find a romance or spy novel concealed inside. It made him like Bastian even more.

May had offered to fully adapt the upstairs flat for him, but Bastian was unconcerned. 'I've lived my whole life this way,' he'd said. 'I'm adaptable, the flat doesn't need to be.' So, apart from purchasing more stepladders, removing the legs from the sofa and armchairs, and lowering the towel hooks and rails, the flat was the same as when May first purchased it.

Fletcher sagged onto the old bookshop sofa beside May, as Bastian made coffee and sliced cake.

'How's David doing?' Bastian asked.

'About as well as can be expected,' Fletcher replied. 'Still in shock.'

'I heard they think it was poison.' Bastian had lowered his voice. 'Darcy popped in earlier.' He placed their drinks and cakes on the low table in front of them. 'Arsenic,' she said. His face was creased with concern.

'Yes, that's what she told me too,' May replied. 'We didn't ask David for details. Too early for that.' She leaned forward to slowly stir her cappuccino.

Fletcher was preparing to take a bite of Bakewell tart. It was a beauty, decorated with thick white icing and glacé cherries. Bastian had recently started purchasing cakes for the shop from the Bluebird Café in Lewisham. Fletcher's waistband was feeling the pressure. The tasty morsel was halfway to his mouth when every mobile phone in the shop dinged, pinged and vibrated. He jumped, sending the bite of cake into his lap.

May reached into her handbag, extracting her phone.

Fletcher swiped at his trousers. Red jam smeared across his thigh. 'Bugger.'

May looked at Bastian. 'Did you get the same message?' she asked.

Bastian held up his screen. 'Shakespeare again, I think,' he said. 'And sent at the same time as yesterday.'

Fletcher looked around the shop in irritation. The customers were all looking at their phones too. 'These trousers are going to have to be dry-cleaned,' he said, scrubbing at the jam. 'What's all this about a text message? Did you get another one?'

'Stop messing about and check your phone,' May said. 'Did you get the text this time too?'

Fletcher, fingers still sticky with jam, reluctantly removed his phone from the breast pocket of his tweed blazer. He extracted his glasses from a separate pocket and put them on. Christ, how could such a small bit of jam spread so far and wide? There was some smeared on his glasses now. He did his best to ignore the mess and squinted at the screen.

A message from an unknown number read:

> Give them great meals of my flesh and blood and bones. They will eat like wolves and die like devils.

'Is that Biblical?' he asked. 'Eucharistic?'

'I think it's a bastardisation of Shakespeare,' Bastian replied, using both thumbs to quickly type on his own phone. 'Yes, here it is. In *Henry V*. "Give them great meals of beef and iron and steel, they will eat like wolves and fight like devils".' He swiped screens to read the message again. 'A strange reworking of the line.'

'It must mean something,' May said. 'Yesterday it was the

text about a manservant, then a manservant dies. Who are the dying devils referred to in this message?'

Fletcher sat up on the sofa and turned to May, all jam forgotten. 'You think the person who sent this message killed Juan? Can we trace it back to them? Find out who sent it?'

Bastian frowned. 'I can try, but it's easy to hide these days. It's not like tracing a call in the past.'

'What are we supposed to do?' Fletcher said.

May shrugged. 'I guess we wait and see who dies tonight.'

CHAPTER NINE

SO TIRED

The following morning Minty was at the table eating her special yoghurt to lower cholesterol and her high fibre cereal to keep her regular, thinking that growing old was a real pain in the backside, when May entered the kitchen scrolling through her phone. The dogs raised their heads from their cushion beside the Aga, saw there were no treats on offer, then lowered them again.

'You young people and your gadgets,' Minty said. 'I thought you were opposed to technology with all your rules about no electronics in your precious library.'

'Not *opposed*,' May said, eyes never leaving the screen. 'Just highly critical.' She sat down at the table, setting the phone aside with a huff. She looked just like she did the time Harold Mortimer inexplicably picked Julie Christiansen over May for the school dance. Poor boy fell through the ice on Blackheath Pond that winter. It's a wonder he survived.

'Bad news?' Minty asked.

'Good news, I suppose,' May said, continuing to look confused and disappointed. Then she stood up and left the kitchen.

Minty glanced at May's phone, discarded on the table. She considered having a look through it, then changed her mind. Minty had other things to think about.

She carefully ticked items off the to-do list in her head.

Spoken to the vicar about my funeral plans. Tick.

Poor Father David wasn't thrilled with some of Minty's arrangements, but he'd come round in the end.

She didn't want hymns at her service, she wanted actual music, something with a decent beat and happy memories. When he'd gently suggested a humanist ceremony at the crematorium might be more fitting, Minty had been scandalised. 'I was born right there,' she said, pointing in the direction of Greenway. 'And my funeral will be held right here.' She pointed at the altar of St Julian's. 'That is the way it has always been for the Morrigans, and the way it will always be.'

Spoken to the funeral home. Tick.

That had been a long and tedious conversation. The funeral director had been appalled when she'd asked to see some of his previous work. Silly man.

'There will be people coming to my funeral who haven't seen me in a very long time,' Minty had explained. 'I need to look my best. Who does the hair and make-up here?'

'I can assure you that we have a very competent person who will see to your needs,' the director had tried to reassure her.

'Where were they trained?' Minty asked. 'I don't want my wig askew or, God forbid, my real hair simply scraped back off my face. And I'd like my wrinkles smoothed out and a tighter neckline. A bit more fullness in the upper cheeks. I understand you can do that sort of thing. Not *too* much cleavage, but at least a peek. My bosoms are one of my finest features. I have a photo for you to work from.'

Minty handed him a glamorous snap taken on the French Riviera in the late 1970s. There was Minty in a long, sheer dress, breasts clearly visible under the diaphanous fabric. She was smiling at the camera with a cigarette in one hand and a martini in the other. He looked from the photo to Minty, then back at the photo. He swallowed audibly.

'I can assure you that you'll look very lovely,' he said.

'I should hope so for the prices you're charging,' Minty said. 'Now, do you have any lavender hearses? And if not, how much would it cost to have one painted for the occasion?'

The details were all in place, yet Minty was no closer to her ultimate goal. Surprisingly, May seemed to have no interest in helping her die. In fact, in the last few days May had been distracted by something going on in the village. She'd hardly responded at all to Minty's digs and criticisms. Perhaps a different tactic was needed. Could she appeal to May's sense of empathy?

May was complicated. She could be tempestuous and had a vile temper, but when she loved someone, it was with equal fervour. Minty was certain that, regardless of appearances, May loved her very deeply. She'd even loved that dreadful, sappy James with all her heart. May had seen and understood him, really *seen* him, and loved him still. The problem was that James didn't want to be seen. He wanted to hide behind some fantasy version of himself, an image that was built on constant external validation. He needed continual praise, wasted money on cars, gadgets, all just *stuff* to try to make himself feel special or important. The truth was that, though May loved him, James Faraday despised himself. In the end, he'd rejected someone who truly loved *him*, warts and all, for someone who accepted the lie. Minty almost pitied him. Almost.

She was consoled by the fact that James could never be truly happy because, though he might be able to fool some people, he would never be able to completely fool himself.

Just like Bertie, always trying to be something that he

wasn't, unable to love himself as he truly was. Minty had never hated Bertie, she'd pitied him, trapped in a prison created by society, though in many ways he'd been his own jailor. Other men like Bertie had found ways to be happy. Minty had known a number of 'confirmed bachelors', but Bertie preferred the charade. He was determined to win the admiration of those who would've condemned him, had they known his secret. To some extent, he'd succeeded, but was the acceptance of a few snooty buffoons worth a lifetime of unhappiness?

Those patterns again. They seemed to be everywhere.

CHAPTER TEN

REBEL REBEL

May sat in her library, a big book open in her lap, reading up on the process for testing a substance for arsenic. Bess and George lolled on their cushion beside her.

Nitric acid... hydrogen peroxide...

She'd set up a small lab in the cellar a few months before, vented through the coal hole, for a different project. It was easy enough to do again. She planned to test the coffee and salts for arsenic later that morning.

As far as May knew, no one had died after the second message. She'd checked the village online discussion groups and the WhatsApp groups on her phone. Most importantly, she'd received no news from Darcy Cooper. Were the text messages unrelated to Juan's death after all?

Regardless of the messages, Juan *had* died from poisoning. The type of poisoning made it almost certainly deliberate. It had to be murder. May couldn't think of any other way that he could ingest a quantity of arsenic large enough to die so quickly.

The dogs raised their heads and sniffed the air, wagging their tails in excitement.

'So, who died?' Barbara Bouvier entered the library,

obviously preceded by the scent of Chanel No. 5. The dogs jumped up and scampered over to have their ears scratched. They hadn't seen Barb for weeks.

Barb was Fletcher's flamboyant alter ego. She'd sashayed into their lives when May and Fletcher lived together at Cambridge in the sixties. Fletcher had been playing Widow Twankey in the Footlights Christmas panto of *Robin Hood*. He started wearing the costume in the privacy of their shared flat, at first to "get into character", then while cooking or pottering about indoors, and eventually Barbara Bouvier was born. When he started writing romance novels to supplement his teaching income, Barb was the obvious choice of author.

'No one died,' May said. 'At least, not that I know of.'

'Don't look so down about it, poppet,' Barb said. 'Someone may be lying in a pool of blood on their kitchen floor even as we speak.'

May smiled. 'What are your plans today? Doing some writing?'

Fletcher had lived a double life since his twenties. Sometimes he was Barb Bouvier, author of bestselling romance novels including *Windy City Wench*, which tells the story of a woman who resorts to prostitution when she loses everything in the Great Chicago Fire of 1871, and *Get Your Rocks Off*, a dual timeline narrative following the lives and loves of a modern-day geologist and a Neolithic farmer, both working at Stonehenge. Barb was flamboyant and fun, had a wicked sense of humour and a wardrobe to die for. Her first novel, *The Whore of Leningrad*, had been written on a whim, but Barb's writing had quickly surpassed all expectations, allowing Fletcher to leisurely pursue his other career as Dr Fletcher Redmond, loved and respected professor of art history. Wearer of silk ascots and tweed, able to tell a Boucher from a Fragonard at forty paces.

May was accustomed to this duality and responded accordingly.

Barb sat on the arm of the sofa, swinging one Gucci-clad leg. 'The latest book seems to have dried up. I just can't get excited about the butcher anymore. I think I'll stick it in the bottom drawer and start something new. I've got this idea for a character who's–'

'A computer science teacher?' May said, thinking of Barb's current lover, Sparks.

Barb pursed her lips. 'No,' she replied. 'Not exactly. I'm thinking he's more of an inventor.' She blushed. May knew very well that Sparks liked to invent gadgets in his spare time. His patent application for laundry tongs was pending.

'I think it sounds like a brilliant idea,' May said. 'And is this inventor's lover a man or a woman?' She'd been encouraging Barb to add a bit more diversity to her plot lines.

Barb rolled her eyes. 'A woman. I don't think Barbara Bouvier's readers are ready for a gay romance.'

'I'm sure you know best,' May said, though in this instance it was quite the opposite. 'How is Sparks getting on at the coast?'

'He's in his element,' Barb said. 'It's all about the bees today. Repairing hives, checking the laying workers, making sure they're feeding properly. He's invented a new pollen feeder and is testing it out. We'll be swimming in honey by the end of the summer.'

May's phone pinged from the shelf outside the library.

'Ooooh, maybe someone's kicked the bucket after all,' Barb said, lounging on the sofa with the dogs. 'Hopefully that Mordecai Page. He gives me the creeps.'

May walked over to the shelf to check her phone. 'Not a death, but there's been another message.' She checked the time. 'Must've arrived at ten again. Bastian is forwarding it over.' Her phone pinged again, then May went very still.

'What does it say?' Barb asked, sitting up in excitement.
May turned the screen towards her.

> God has given you one face and you make
> yourself a woman. Put away the dresses.
> You're fooling no one. FR

'I think this one's for you,' May said.

CHAPTER ELEVEN

GET READY

As the sun was setting over the heath, the temperature dropped and the clouds rolled in. Spring was such a tease.

May was at the drinks trolley in the library preparing a martini for Minty. Bastian was on the settee sipping his cranberry juice, while Fletcher paced around the room, jiggling the ice in his empty glass.

'FR, it says. That must be me. Can you think of any other FRs in the village?' he said. Ever the drama queen.

'Give me your glass.' May held out her hand. 'I think you need another drink. I'll make this one a double.'

Minty had taken her own drink and was perched in an armchair, feet resting on a footstool. She looked delighted with all the excitement, big eyes moving from person to person, a dachshund tucked under each arm.

'There may be other FRs,' Bastian said. 'But the references to dresses and being a woman does seem to conclusively point to you, Fletch.'

'Christ on a bike,' he said, sitting down next to Bastian. 'Does this mean some deranged person is after me? Am I going to be poisoned?' He looked at his drink, then set it down on the table.

'Oh, for goodness' sake.' May picked up Fletcher's glass, took a big swig, then placed it back in his hand. 'No poison,' she said. 'Except the good kind. I cleared out the kitchen this morning, removing anything that could've been tampered with. Such a dreadful waste, but I don't want to take any chances.'

May sat in her armchair, arranging her Celia Birtwell skirt carefully. She'd recently been shopping for spring dresses and was delighted with the brightly coloured floral. From her handbag she retrieved a stack of paper. 'I've written up some notes,' she said, distributing pages to everyone, including Minty.

The library fell silent as each of them read through May's notes. The only sounds were the spring rain against the library windows and George's low growl of pleasure as she yawned in Minty's lap.

First message:

> Some rise by sin. I know all about the unnatural acts you commit with your manservant. DP
>
> Measure for Measure, said by Escalus in Act 2, Scene 1:
>
> 'Well, heaven forgive him! and forgive us all!
> Some rise by sin, and some by virtue fall.'
>
> DP = David Panagos? But Juan was the one who was killed.

Second message:

>   Give them great meals of my flesh and blood and
> bones. They will eat like wolves and die like devils.
>   Henry V, said by Constable in Act 3, Scene 7:
>   'And then give them great meals of beef and iron
> and steel,
>   They will eat like wolves and fight like devils.'
>   No initials. No one was injured or died, that we
> know of so far.

Third message:

>   God has given you one face and you make yourself
> a woman. Put away the dresses. You're fooling no
> one. FR
>   Hamlet, said by Hamlet to Ophelia in Act 3,
> Scene 1:
>   'God has giv-
> en you one face, and you make yourself another.
>   You jig, you amble, and you lisp, and
> nickname God's creatures,
>   and make your wantonness your ignorance.'
>   FR = Fletcher Redmond?

'This is just a collection of data,' May said. 'I'm not sure what matters and what doesn't. If we step back from the situation, we have to ask ourselves if the texts are linked to Juan's death at all. To me, it seems too much of a coincidence that we started receiving the messages at the same time that someone mentioned in them dies.'

'I agree,' Fletcher said. He looked at the page he was holding. 'Seeing it laid out like this, why are there no initials on the second text? Is that important?'

'Perhaps just sloppy,' Minty said. 'Killers can't all be organised and efficient.' She winked at May.

'Have you been able to trace the number?' May asked Bastian, studiously ignoring Minty.

He shook his head. 'Each message was sent from a different number, and they all seem to be burner phones, cheap phones not linked to a contract or person. Or, if the person is tech-savvy, they could be using a burner app, which would create the same effect.'

'Why would they use different numbers?' May asked.

'I suppose it could be in case we blocked the number after receiving a message,' Bastian replied. 'Whoever's sending these messages, he or she wants them to be seen.'

'And why ten o'clock each morning, is that significant?' Fletcher said.

Bastian shrugged. 'I suppose it could have meaning to the sender, but it's not immediately obvious to me.'

'I had a quick look into the possible significance of the time,' May said. 'I couldn't find anything specifically related to 10am historically, but it's referred to as the "triple hour" or "mirror hour" in certain belief systems. It's related to guardian angels guiding their charges to success. Complete nonsense, but I assume that whoever is sending these messages isn't an emotionally balanced person.'

'And what about the quotes?' Fletcher said. 'Were they chosen because they were convenient, or is there a deeper relevance to the characters and situations in the plays? That extended quote used in the third message certainly sounds like Barb.'

May gave a weary sigh. 'I read through the plays this afternoon and I can't see any deeper meaning. The quote used in the second message is about preparing an army for battle. I'm not sure the context is relevant.'

'It shows they know their Shakespeare,' Minty said, holding her empty glass out to May, who took it and moved to make another drink.

'That's true,' May said, forehead creasing. 'None of them are terribly famous lines. Not something the average person would know off the top of their head.' Her afternoon scouring Shakespeare had reminded May how indifferent she was to the Bard. His popularity was a continuing mystery to her.

'But anyone with access to the internet could find them in seconds,' Bastian pointed out. 'Did you have any luck in the lab today?'

'Yes.' May perked up. 'Nothing in the Andrews Salts, but there was a whack of arsenic in the coffee pod. I couldn't tell you exactly how much, but it was there.'

Bastian looked thoughtful. 'Coffee can contain traces of arsenic. Can you tell if it was more than a trace?'

'Not in any measurable sense with the basic lab I have to work with, but it was enough to be immediately apparent. Much more than a trace, I should think,' May replied, handing the martini to Minty. 'The most telling detail was that the foil lid of the pod had been cut open and resealed, right on the edge. It was carefully done and could easily be overlooked. Someone doctored that pod with arsenic.'

'Could it have been done in the factory?' Fletcher asked.

'It's been known to happen. There was that terrible incident in the States in the early eighties with paracetamol tampering. May and I were in Chicago at the time. It was dreadful. People were terrified they were going to be poisoned by anything in a package.'

'It's possible,' Bastian said. 'But I think if someone was doing that, there would be other deaths. It wouldn't be just the one.'

'That means that someone had access to the coffee pods,' May said, resuming her seat. 'Could it have been in the shop and it's just a malicious individual rather than a targeted poisoning?' She thought it over, then answered her own question. 'But that wouldn't link to the texts and, as you pointed out, in a situation like that there would probably be other deaths. It seems more likely it was someone who had the time and opportunity to place the poisoned pods in the cabinet, knowing that only Juan used the Nespresso.' She looked at Fletcher. 'Would David do such a thing? He'll be the most obvious suspect.'

'No.' Fletcher shook his head with decision. 'I can't believe he would ever harm Juan.'

'It's the vicarage,' Bastian said. 'People are in and out of there all the time. The volunteers, the church wardens, anyone from the parish stopping in for a chat. Any of them would have the opportunity, though few would have access to arsenic.'

'Someone from the church might have all of our mobile numbers too,' May added. 'There's a contact sheet in the crypt kitchen with details for half the village. I wonder if we could cross-reference that list against anyone who's received the texts. It might prove the sender is linked to St Julian's.'

'I bet it's that Mordecai Page,' Fletcher said. 'He looks like a serial killer. Does the man ever wash?'

'Mordecai?' Minty said, sitting forward. 'Is he still alive? Oh my days, I could tell you some stories about Mordecai Page.'

'What sort of stories?' Fletcher asked with trepidation. 'Do I want to know?'

'We called him the Hobby Horse,' Minty replied with a twinkle in her eye. 'Because everyone wanted a ride and he was hung like–'

'All right!' May interjected. 'We get it. I don't see how that's relevant to this discussion.'

Minty rolled her eyes in response.

'Marcia Jackson!' Fletcher said, sitting up on the sofa, almost dropping his glass. 'I'd completely forgotten about her.'

'Who's Marcia Jackson?' May asked. She and Bastian turned towards Fletcher. Minty stirred her drink with a finger, lost in her bawdy old memories.

'It was Minty talking about stories that reminded me. When I came home yesterday morning there was a young journalist in front of the house. She asked if I'd been living a double life as Barbara Bouvier. She was writing a story on the subject. I can't believe I'd forgotten about her.' Fletcher shook his head, eyebrows high on his forehead. 'Juan's death just blotted everything else out.' He was silent for a moment, gathering his thoughts before continuing. 'There've been lots of theories about Barb, that she's a pen name for some literary author or that her books are written by a consortium, but she's never been linked to me personally before. That's new.' He looked at May. 'Might that be my "punishment"? Exposure rather than death?'

'David's initials were on the text, but David didn't die. If we're thinking of it as punishment, I guess his punishment was losing Juan,' May said. Her eyebrows came together. 'I suppose, at a stretch, one could argue that exposure would mean you "losing" Barb.' She pursed her lips. 'Pretty tame in comparison though.'

Bastian was listening and nodding slowly. 'And what about

the second text?' he asked. 'Who was punished after that one was sent?'

May shrugged.

Fletcher slumped back in his seat. 'I feel more muddled than I did when we started,' he said. 'We're looking for someone familiar with Shakespeare, with access to the vicarage, a supply of arsenic, a belief in guardian angels, knowledge of burner phones and all of our phone numbers. Strangely enough, no one springs to mind.'

Bastian set his empty glass on the table. 'I think the arsenic could be the weak point,' he said. 'As May pointed out, Shakespeare quotes can be googled. The person could also look up how to disguise a phone number. It's really not that difficult. The most revealing points are access to the vicarage and the arsenic. If you wanted arsenic, how would you go about it?'

'It's naturally occurring,' May said. 'One can find traces of it in everything from seafood to drinking water. Extracting it to a lethal level is very difficult to do on one's own. Or so I've been told.'

'I did a little research this afternoon,' Bastian said. 'It's used in metal-refining, glass-making and mining. These are all industrial uses. I don't suppose we know anyone who works in those industries?'

May and Fletcher shook their heads.

'Fowler's Solution,' Minty piped up. They turned to look at her. 'My father used to take it regularly. Said it was the only thing that helped his psoriasis. Apparently full of arsenic, but very popular.'

'Didn't grandfather die of bladder cancer?' May asked.

'Yes,' Minty replied. 'Had one of those horrible little bags for years after surgery. Mother would empty it for him throughout the day.' She placed her hand on the little table beside her. 'Touch wood. At least I've been spared such indignities.'

'Thankfully, Fowler's Solution no longer exists,' Fletcher said. 'What about rat poison, doesn't that contain arsenic?'

'It used to,' Bastian said. 'So did weed killer and ant killer, but not since the mid-twentieth century.'

'As late as the fifties?' May asked. 'I've probably got rat poison or weed killer older than that in the cellar, as will anyone who has an old home. It gets pushed to the back of a shelf and just stays there for decades.'

Fletcher nodded. 'Sparks said that when his family bought the house on the coast, the previous owners left a load of stuff in an outbuilding. Some of it was machinery that he was able to repurpose, but there were various poisonous substances too. His father had to arrange for some specialists to dispose of it all.'

'If we exclude anyone living in a newer home,' Bastian said, 'that includes the Span houses around the Cator Estate, the homes that were built on bomb-sites after the war and anyone who lives in a new development of flats.' He shook his head. 'It doesn't narrow the field by much. Most of Blackheath is Victorian up to pre-war. Apart from the vicarage, everyone I can think of off the top of my head lives in a period home.'

They went back over all the information again as Minty dozed off in her chair, snoring even more loudly than the dogs.

CHAPTER TWELVE

HOLD ON, I'M COMIN'

A s the discussion about the mysterious messenger started to go round in circles, Fletcher saw May slowly shrink in her chair. He'd noticed that she'd become quieter in the last week. His time with Sparks was special, but he realised that he'd been neglecting his dearest friend. If May was focussed on finding out who was sending the text messages, then he would throw himself into the project wholeheartedly. He just wasn't sure where to begin.

Bastian stood and began to gather his things. 'If some "devil" was supposed to die after that second text, it seems like it didn't come off.'

They walked into the entry hall where May said her goodbyes, then returned to the library to wake Minty.

Bastian looked at Fletcher. 'You could be right about the journalist being your punishment.' He reached up to grasp Fletcher's shoulder. 'But you could be wrong. Just stay safe and don't do anything silly.'

'Of course not,' Fletcher replied with a catch in his voice. Bastian saluted, then sauntered off into the wet night.

Fletcher remained at the door, admiring the soft, velvety

evening atmosphere. The misty rain sparkled in halos around each streetlight, it's gentle pitter-patter could be heard dripping from the eaves. It was fresh and damp on the heath, but summer was on its way. The evenings were already getting brighter. In a few months it would be light well into the evening and the heath would be covered with merrymakers, worshipping the sun as their ancestors did before them. *Semper et in aeternum.*

In the library there was a loud crash, a thud and the sound of breaking glass.

'Bloody hell!' May shouted.

Fletcher ran back into the room to find Minty on the floor, the drinks trolley on its side and May on her final straw.

'What happened?' he said, rushing to Minty's side. 'Are you injured?'

'She's fine,' May said. 'Just hammered. I was trying to help her out of the chair when she keeled over onto the trolley. Careful! There's broken glass everywhere.' She snatched up the dogs and carried them out of the room.

Minty moaned, face down on the floor.

'What did you say?' Fletcher leaned closer.

Minty moaned again, this time with more force.

Fletcher leaned even closer. 'Say it once more,' he said.

'I said, I'VE BROKEN MY FUCKING HIP!' Minty shouted as she attempted to roll over, then collapsed back into position with a groan. 'Call the bloody ambulance. NOW!'

She sounded so much like May, Fletcher almost laughed. Instead, he backed away and collected his phone from the shelf outside the library door.

'You haven't broken your hip,' May said, returning without the dogs. 'You didn't even *bump* your hip. You went face forwards. And in slow motion, I might add. It was like watching the Six Million Dollar Man jump out of an extremely low-flying helicopter.' She started collecting the biggest bits of glass from the floor and placing them in a napkin.

Fletcher saw that he'd received a text from David. It would have to wait.

'Oh, for God's sake. I think I know what I've done.' Minty looked like a bug stuck on its back, except she was stuck on her stomach, face down on the Turkish rug. 'Just ring for the shitting ambulance,' she shouted, her voice muffled by the carpet.

'You heard her, Fletcher. Ring the shitting ambulance!' May mocked.

'I'm ringing the shitting ambulance right now!' Fletcher said.

Over an hour later, Fletcher collapsed into a library chair, exhausted. They'd waited half an hour for the ambulance to arrive with May and Minty bickering the whole time.

'It was like watching a less graceful, geriatric version of *The Matrix*...'

'You won't be laughing when you're changing my nappies tomorrow...'

Once they'd finally left for the hospital, he'd set about sweeping, hoovering and mopping up the spilled spirits and broken glass. At last, the library was put to rights.

His phone pinged, May texting to say that Minty was being examined. Fletcher suddenly remembered the unread text from David. He saw that there was more than one:

> Please come at once.

> It's unbearable.

> I'm afraid I might do something silly.

Fletcher grabbed a jacket and was out the door.

Once outside, he hesitated, realising the streetlight in front of the house wasn't working, making it unusually dark.

Don't be a silly sod.

But which would be more foolish: being too afraid to go to a friend in need? Or walking alone in the dark when there was a possible murderer about?

Checking his watch, he saw that it was after ten o'clock. Perhaps he'd ring David instead.

No. David had specifically asked him to come. Fletcher refused to let a friend down. He already felt guilty for the delay in reading the messages. It was just a quick walk across the heath, through the village, and the vicarage was less than a hundred metres on the other side. It would be fine.

He quickly texted David.

On my way.

Fletcher took a deep breath and set off.

The heath was dark, a new-moon night. The rain had stopped, leaving the air heavy with a fine mist. Sadly, or in this case, fortunately, the London light pollution meant that he could still see enough to know that there was no one about in the open space. Making a beeline for the village, only a scavenging fox crossed Fletcher's path along the way.

Once in the safe harbour of Blackheath Village, he berated himself for ever hesitating. The pubs were still open, and the restaurants were closing, spilling bright light and dawdlers out onto the pavement. It was almost jolly. Fletcher hurried along, nodding good evening to familiar faces. By the time he was climbing the hill at the opposite end of the village, he'd almost forgotten that he could be in danger.

Just halfway down Lee Park and he would be at David's. The vicarage was on a leafy, residential road, tall trees creating a lofty tunnel. Lined with a mix of Victorian and Georgian homes, along with the popular Span development, driveways opened off both sides of the street with the occasional alleyway creating a shortcut to the surrounding roads. He and May had walked there many times, often cutting through an alley on their way to Manor House Gardens or Halcyon Books on the High Road. It was all very familiar, yet something about the silence made it feel strangely sinister.

Fletcher ploughed onward until the creeping feeling in his gut caused him to slow, then stop, and raise his head to listen. He could hear cars passing at the top of the road, laughter and voices in the village. So much life being lived close by, but here under the trees it was oddly hushed. The only sounds were the dripping of water and the rustling branches overhead.

He felt the hair rise on the back of his neck. Goosebumps prickled on his forearms. Fletcher held his breath. Then, beside him in the black of an alley, a twig snapped.

Fletcher managed to spin away just as the knife descended. He glimpsed a figure in black, felt the thrust of the blade, then heard the attacker sprinting away back up the alley.

Breathing hard, he leaned against a tree to catch his breath. It had all happened so quickly. The shock was causing him to shiver when something moved at the corner of his eye. He turned to look and saw the handle of the knife still protruding from his right shoulder.

'Oh, for fuck's sa–' he slurred.

Then all was darkness.

CHAPTER THIRTEEN

BABY LOVE

May pushed Minty through the hospital in a wheelchair. 'I knew you hadn't broken your hip,' May said. 'You're barely bruised.'

'That doctor was virtually a foetus,' Minty replied. 'I don't know how they're allowed to practise so young.'

'And his age makes him unable to tell a broken bone from a bruise?'

'Just take me home. I've had a trying evening,' Minty grumbled. 'Paracetamol and an ice pack... Useless.'

As they came around the corner, there was a flurry of activity as a patient was wheeled through the doors of A & E. He was sitting upright and forward, carefully keeping the knife jutting out from one shoulder away from the back of the wheelchair.

'Fletcher!' May shouted.

He instinctively turned towards her voice, then yelped as the knife handle made contact with the chair.

'Oh my God,' May said. 'What are you doing here?' She trundled over with Minty.

'I was feeling a bit under the weather,' he replied.

'What?' May said, confused. 'Really?'

'No, not really,' he spat. 'Have you failed to notice the bloody great knife sticking out of my fucking back?' In his agitation, the handle smacked into the back of the chair again, causing Fletcher to squawk. He clamped his lips together and closed his eyes.

The knife looked like an old steak knife with a worn wooden handle. Probably covered in dirt and germs that were doing more damage than the laceration. May blanched at the thought. The blade wasn't very big and there was minimal blood visible on Fletcher's jacket. Still, must be agony.

'Christ on a bike, can someone get this fucking thing out of me?' Fletcher turned towards the medics who'd brought him in.

'Yes, sir,' one of them replied. 'Just getting you checked in. They'll have you sorted in no time.'

'Thank you,' Fletcher replied, slightly mollified. 'Apologies for swearing. I'm in a great deal of pain.'

'No worries,' the young man replied with a wink. 'I've heard worse from my own granny.'

Fletcher looked at May as the young medic walked back towards the waiting ambulance. 'What do you suppose he meant by that? His granny? How old does he think I am?'

'I can see death isn't exactly imminent,' May replied with a wry smile.

'I saw that wink,' Minty said. 'I think you're in there, Fletch.'

May was back and forth from Greenway to the hospital throughout the night. First, ferrying Minty home to bed, then at Fletcher's insistence, going to check on David.

Father David, still half asleep, answered May's knock at the vicarage door. He'd been sleeping in his clothes, his hair standing on end and his breath reeking of booze. 'I'm fine,' he said, blinking and attempting to focus on May's face. 'What time is it?'

'It's after midnight,' May said. 'I'm so sorry to disturb you. Fletcher was worried about some texts you'd sent him earlier this evening.'

'Texts?' David yawned and scratched, causing May to shrink away from the stench. 'I don't think I texted Fletcher but, to be honest, I've had a bit too much to drink this evening.'

When May explained the events of the night, David insisted on returning to the hospital with her. She arrived with fresh clothes for Fletcher and a tipsy vicar, then made another run home and back again when the outfit she'd chosen for Fletcher wasn't up to spec.

Fletcher was released a few hours later, just as the sun was coming up over Blackheath.

'I can't believe they *cut* the jacket off me. It was Belstaff!' Fletcher said as May helped him into his bed. 'Honestly, what is the world coming to?'

He'd been very lucky. Fletcher's reflexes had saved him. If he hadn't turned when he did, the knife would've most likely ended up in his heart.

'What else could they do?' May asked. 'You'd be more upset if they'd tried to winkle the jacket off around the knife. Imagine that filthy blade wobbling about in the wound, wiggling back and forth while they tried to thread it through the jacket and then the shirt.'

'Yes, all right. I get the point,' Fletcher said, grimacing at May's description. 'It's a bloody nuisance, all the same.'

He'd returned home with antibiotics, painkillers and a tidy set of stitches in his shoulder.

'You're going to have a charming scar and a thrilling story. And, most importantly, you've lived to tell the tale,' May soothed. 'That's worth more than any old jacket. Sparks will be here later with soup and treats. I told him you needed to rest this morning.'

Fletcher perked up at the thought of Sparks. He reached out to take May's hand as she smoothed the duvet over him. 'Thank you,' he said.

'What for?' May asked. 'It's that dog walker you should be thanking. It was fortunate she saw the whole thing and rang 999. And had enough sense not to pull the knife out.'

He was lying on his side, keeping the sore shoulder elevated. 'I know. But thank you... for being my family.'

May leaned forward and kissed his forehead. 'We're better than family,' she said. 'We actually like each other.'

Fletcher chuckled, but stopped immediately as it caused him to jiggle the wound. He peered into May's face.

'You need to get some rest too,' he said. 'I did at least manage to doze at the hospital. David wittered on for a bit about wickedness in the world, then thankfully passed out in his chair.'

May looked at the bedside clock. 'I'm popping over to the shop first. I want to see if another message arrives today. This is personal now.' She looked back at Fletcher. 'I'm determined to catch the bastard.'

Fletcher smiled. 'Give me twenty-four hours and I'll be right there with you.'

His eyes were already closing when May slipped out of the room.

She poked her head into Minty's bedroom where, unusually, Minty was still sleeping. May stopped to watch her mother's chest rise and fall a few times. At Minty's age, it was wise to make sure.

Then May texted Betty Danvers to delay her usual morning visit. Minty needed her rest too.

She decided to take the dogs to the shop with her. They'd had an unsettled night with all the comings and goings. A good walk would ensure they slept well. She scratched their ears and rubbed Bess's proffered belly as she slipped on their harnesses. The dogs wriggled in delight.

May assumed that having dogs was not unlike having young children with their routines, naps, playtime and bedtime. Sadly, May had never had any children of her own, though she'd wanted to. James always had a reason why they should wait a little longer, just a bit longer, until finally there was no time left. He'd denied her the family she'd longed for, while keeping a secret family of his own. Why had he bothered to stay with May for so long?

The bigger mystery was why *she'd* stayed with him. Why had she tolerated such treatment? If she was brutally honest with herself, May knew that she'd probably still be with James today if he hadn't been the one to leave. Would she be happier now if he'd stayed? She mentally slapped herself. Of course she wouldn't. She had Greenway, the dogs, Fletcher. After the initial shock had worn off, she couldn't deny that she'd actually been much happier since James left.

Christ, her exhaustion was making her gloomy. She stood up, shedding the cloud of uncertainty. The walk and fresh air would do May some good as well.

It was a beautiful day. The heath was a vibrant green after the rain, buzzing with dogs and small children. The sun warmed May's skin, though the breeze was still cool. Soon enough the grass would be a brittle yellow as the increasingly uncomfortable summer heat reached its peak.

At the bookshop, May was surprised to find she could barely squeeze through the door. The place was packed. She released Bess and George from their leads. They weaved their way through the forest of legs to their cushion beside the radiator as May made her way over to Bastian.

'What's going on?' she said.

'I think it's the text messages,' Bastian replied. 'I've asked around and it seems that no one receives them unless they're in the shop. The good news is we're making a killing on coffees and teas. No one is shameless enough to just stand around in here, waiting for the show to start. How's Fletch doing?'

May looked around at the people pretending to browse. As Bastian had said, everyone had a cup of something in one hand, their mobile phone in the other. Jilly, May's cleaner, helped out in the shop sometimes. She was in the room at the back, selling drinks and the few remaining cakes. May's neighbour, Geoffrey, was lurking in the spiritualist section. She hoped The Cretin wasn't finding religion. He was insufferable enough already.

Betty had detoured to the shop where she and Jean Drysdale were installed in two armchairs, deep in conversation. Even Nick, the new village butcher, was there, flipping through a copy of *The Carnivore Cookbook*.

'I'm pleased to say that Fletcher will be fine,' May said. 'After the loving attention and ministrations of Sparks, he'll be more than fine.' She scanned the room, alert for thumbs hitting the send button. 'Do you think we have any chance of spotting who's sending these messages?'

'Not much,' Bastian replied. 'Still, we can but try.' He sipped his green tea and surveyed the room with May.

As ten o'clock drew closer, there was a growing sense of tension in the shop. Voices were lowered. Browsers grew still. Then, just as the bells of St Julian's started to ring out the hour, the bubble of anticipation burst into satisfaction as phones began to beep, buzz and chime.

May looked at Bastian. 'Did you see anything?' she asked.

He shook his head. 'Every other person was on their phone. Impossible to tell.'

May removed her phone from her handbag and checked the screen. There it was.

> It's a foolish father that doesn't know his own child. We all know little Clemmie isn't really yours. LK

There was a cry from the rear of the shop. Jean Drysdale was on her feet, her face flushed with anger. 'Who sent this?' she shouted, waving her phone in the air. 'Why would anyone say such a thing? This is absurd.'

Jean's daughter had recently given birth to Jean's first grandchild, Clementine Kirkland.

CHAPTER FOURTEEN

YOU NEVER CAN TELL

May and Bastian pushed through the crowd to Jean's side, then herded her towards the door to the flat upstairs.

'Jilly, can you watch the shop for a bit?' Bastian asked. Jilly nodded, looking surprised and slightly dazed.

'Who would say such a horrible thing?' Jean was furious, but she allowed May and Bastian to lead her up to Bastian's sitting room. He disappeared to the kitchen where May could hear him filling the kettle and rattling china.

'Come sit down,' May said to Jean, who was pacing back and forth. 'Let's talk this through.'

'Oh, hello.' A young woman came out of one of the bedrooms, surprising the women. Her dark hair was still damp from the shower. 'I thought you were Bastian.'

'And who might you be?' May asked. Bastian had a number of admirers, but this was a new face.

'I'm Erika. Erika Lovelace.'

'You're a relative of Bastian's?' May said. How intriguing. He was always a bit mysterious about his past, rarely talked about his family.

'You could say that,' Erika replied, a cheeky smile on her face. 'I'm his wife.'

'Bastian's...?' May sat down hard on the sofa, mouth open.

Jean stepped forward, hand outstretched, her good manners prevailing. 'I'm Jean,' she said. 'It's a pleasure to meet you.'

May popped up to standing again, feeling blindsided, still processing the information. 'It seems congratulations are in order,' she said. 'We had no idea that he... and you... and we're...' May's voice trailed off. 'Congratulations!' She kissed Erika on both cheeks.

Erika smiled, her cheeks pink with pleasure or from the hot shower, May wasn't sure which. 'I'm just popping out for a few things,' Erika said. 'I'll leave you to it. It was lovely to meet you.' She collected a handbag from beside the door, leaving May and Jean staring at each other in the sitting room.

'Well, that was unexpected,' May said.

'You didn't know?' Jean asked.

'Not a clue,' May replied, shaking her head in wonder. Did Darcy Cooper know about the marriage yet? If so, why hadn't she told May?

Jean glanced at her phone, as if fearing another disturbing message would appear.

'Let's sit down and talk about this message,' May said. 'We'll quiz Bastian later.'

Jean hesitated before deciding to sit upright on the edge of an armchair. May sat back down on the sofa across from her.

'You know about the other messages?' May asked.

Jean nodded in reply.

'One thing that's struck me about them,' May said, 'is that they've each contained at least a grain of truth. The sentiments might reflect a narrow personal opinion, but the details have been accurate enough.'

Jean looked at May. 'Really?' She seemed surprised by this information. Her face went crimson.

'Please don't think I'm prying,' May said. 'Whatever you say will never leave this room, I promise you that. Is there any truth to this latest text?'

Jean took a deep breath, looked away, then closed her eyes and nodded slowly. 'It's not what it sounds like though,' she said. 'Charlotte was struggling to get pregnant. She and Louis did endless tests and realised the issue was Louis's sperm count. Very low, lack of motility and all the rest. They made the decision to use a donor.' She read the text message again. 'I suppose that means this is technically true.'

Bastian came in with three mugs of tea. 'I've put some sugar in yours,' he said, handing a mug to Jean. 'It's good for the shock.'

Both women stared at him as he took a seat on the sofa beside May. He looked from one to the other before asking, 'Who else knew about the sperm donor?'

'No one,' Jean said. 'Louis is sensitive about it. We were all sworn to secrecy. I'm surprised they told *us*.'

May nodded, deep in thought. 'I don't want to alarm you,' she said, 'but you know that Juan died after the text about a manservant? Last night Fletcher was stabbed after the message with his initials was received.'

May could almost see the cogs turning in Jean's head as her expression went from bewilderment to realisation to alarm. 'I need to get home,' she said, placing her mug on the table and standing up. 'I need to speak to Louis and Charlotte.' She looked down at May and Bastian, still seated on the sofa. 'Do you really think their lives could be in danger?' Jean sat down again. 'Saying it out loud, it just sounds insane.'

May nodded. 'It does sound mad, but there's no harm in taking them away for a few days. Just to be cautious. Someone stabbed Fletcher with a steak knife last night. It wasn't an attempted mugging. He still had his wallet and watch on him.'

'Whoever is doing this is local,' Bastian said. 'Take your family to the coast for a few days. And do it *today*. They killed Juan and tried to kill Fletcher within hours of the texts going out. Don't let someone in your family be next.'

CHAPTER FIFTEEN

I'M MAKING BELIEVE

Minty stretched in the wide bed, listening to the pop of each extended joint. Her bedroom had once been Bertie's office. She could picture him over beside the fireplace, shouting into a black Bakelite telephone, sitting at the oak desk that May used in her library. Back then the room was all dark green with heavy tartan curtains. It had suited Bertie and his dark moods.

When May took over the house, she'd brightened up the space and turned it into a sitting room. Minty guessed it was last decorated sometime in the mid-eighties. The pastel colours, swag curtains and chintzy fabrics were a dead giveaway. Interesting that May hadn't felt the need to decorate since then. Apart from the library, the whole house was a bit of a time capsule. Minty had been surprised to see the kitchen almost unchanged since she'd last renovated it in the forties. Greenway had become a monument to the moment when May's happiness and hopes for the future began to fade.

Minty rolled over to look at the photo of herself on the bedside table. In her mind she reached out to hold her darling's hand. When she gazed at the photograph, she felt most connected to him, seeing herself through his eyes. That was the real Minty, the laughing girl with the sun on her face and the secret growing in her belly. All of the Mintys who came after her were just hollow versions of the original. She would give anything to be that girl again, so full of love and hope. So whole. A few weeks later, he would be missing, presumed dead. Minty's one chance for true happiness had died along with him.

She rolled back onto the pillows, releasing the memories, and touched her hip to check for pain. It was fine. That little charade with the drinks trolley hadn't worked as well as she'd hoped. Minty had thought that if she couldn't push May to kill her in anger, perhaps she could convince May to kill her in sympathy. The fall had been an attempt to illustrate her physical frailty. Granted, it had not been wholly successful.

Minty and May had knocked heads almost from the day May was born. The arguments over what May would and would not eat, what she could and could not wear. And the teen years when every little thing seemed to be a life or death situation. It was a wonder that they'd both survived. Minty had never imagined that convincing May to kill her would be such hard work.

She'd read about something in the States called 'suicide by cop'. The idea was to commit a small crime, then when the police arrived, wave a gun around and threaten to shoot them. It was a way of committing suicide without pulling the trigger oneself. Apparently popular when one's life insurance contained a non-payment clause for suicide. Buying a gun in American would be a breeze, but she was an elderly white woman. They'd probably just arrest her. Minty didn't imagine that an American prison would be much fun.

Somehow, she'd find a way to talk May around. It would just take time. But first... pleasure.

She sat up and looked at herself in the mirror across the

room. Christ, what a fright. The little hair she had left was standing up in witchy peaks, pink scalp gleaming in between. Minty used her hands to gently pull the loose skin back from her face and neck, turning this way and that to admire the effect.

There she was, the girl she used to be.

It was comforting to know that the bones of Minty remained the same. Under all the damage and dilapidation, Araminta Morrigan still existed unchanged. Inside the old woman, resided the young one, the one who had endured so much, but still knew how to have a really good time.

She let go, allowing the wrinkles and jowls to drop back into place.

'I'd need a roller blind on the back of my head to keep all this loose skin tight these days,' she grumbled before falling back against the pillows.

A bit of paint and perfume, some good underwear and her best wig would do the trick. They'd never failed her before. Men were such simple creatures really.

Poor Bertie. As long as she'd kept the children quiet and had dinner on the table every evening, he was satisfied. With hindsight she could see that he really didn't ask for much, as long as Minty continued to provide the window dressing to his charade of a life. It was when she dared to stray from the script that Bertie's temper was released, leaving destruction in its path.

They'd shared a home, a family, for decades, but Minty felt she'd never really known her husband. In the little that she did know, there was not a great deal to admire.

He'd allowed her parents to stay at Greenway. That was kind. He'd accepted the children as his own, but that had served his own purposes. They'd been part of the disguise along with the beautiful home and lovely wife.

He'd been generous, never complaining about anything that

Minty spent on herself or the girls. He'd asked very little from Minty. The problem was that he also gave very little in return. Her marriage to Bertie had been a lonely one. Bertie disliked her socialising without him, but he wasn't good company, so the flow of invitations eventually dwindled to nothing.

Minty had never really reacquired the skill of making friends. She had lots of acquaintances, plenty of people to visit and dine with, but no true friends. Not like May and Fletcher.

She'd been sitting on the small terrace of her house in Antibes, when she realised that she was done with living. It had been no lightning bolt, no revelation, just a passing thought that had become a gentle certainty. She'd put down the magazine she was reading and thought of Greenway. It would make sense to die there. Full circle and all that. By that afternoon, Minty had supervised the packing of her trunks and booked the flight. It was only when she was locking her front door for the final time that she considered contacting her crowd in Antibes to let them know that she was leaving, never to return.

She got into the taxi without telling a soul. For a while they might wonder what had happened to the funny old English lady, but Minty knew they would soon find someone else to take her place.

CHAPTER SIXTEEN

WE CAN WORK IT OUT

That evening, May, Minty, Fletcher, Sparks and Bastian gathered in May's library to discuss the latest developments.

As soon as she got home, May had told Fletcher all about meeting Bastian's surprise wife. She was frustrated that she hadn't had a chance to quiz Bastian for any details as he'd rushed off to deal with some minor emergency in the shop. Erika hadn't returned before May left for home.

'Why hasn't he said anything?' Fletcher asked.

May shrugged. 'Maybe he wants to keep it a secret for some reason. He'll tell us when he's ready. Until then...' she motioned zipping her mouth shut and throwing away the key, then waggled a finger at Fletcher, 'that includes you too.'

Fletcher hated keeping secrets. His face always seemed to give him away. He fidgeted as he and Sparks waited in the library.

'Are you sure you shouldn't be in bed?' Sparks asked, resting one hand on his knee.

Fletcher, wearing pyjamas and a silk dressing gown with his right arm in a sling, placed his free hand on top of Sparks's and gave it a squeeze. 'I'm sure. I've slept all day and I feel much better. I need to find out who attacked me last night. May has a way of winkling out the truth.'

Sparks's bearded face hardened like an angry Santa Claus. 'Oh, we'll find out,' he said. 'And they'll pay for hurting you.' Fletcher was abruptly aware of the broad, intimidating body that encased Sparks's gentle heart. He'd been a prop on his university's rugby team and had maintained the physique. Fletcher felt a little flutter of desire. Sparks must have noticed because he leaned forward for a gentle but enthusiastic kiss.

'Break it up, you two,' Minty said, rattling the newly filled drinks trolley into the library. 'Old lady coming through. My heart can't take the sight of such debauchery.' She was wearing a becoming green dress and had obviously taken special care with her hair and make-up for the occasion.

Fletcher felt himself blushing as Sparks chuckled beside him.

'I'm sure you've participated in your own fair share of debauchery over the years,' Sparks said, standing to help Minty with the drinks.

She nodded, looking wistful. 'Oh, yes. I've had plenty of fun.' Her face became more serious. 'Not much more than fun, though.' She looked at the men. 'You're lucky. Lust with love is an intoxicating combination, almost as strong as blood.'

'Did someone say lust?' Bastian asked, entering the library with his satchel in one hand and the two dogs trotting behind him. He backtracked to place his phone on the shelf outside the door.

'Minty was just pointing out the power of lust, love and family,' Fletcher said. 'Though not all at the same time.'

Bastian paused to consider. Fletcher watched as his expression changed from contemplation to something resembling pain. 'Yes,' he replied at last. 'Each is very powerful indeed.' He moved over to the drinks trolley to prepare his usual glass of cranberry juice, adding an unexpected splash of vodka. Had married life already driven him to drink?

Fletcher glanced at Bastian's ring finger. No wedding band. Other than looking a bit tired, he seemed the same as ever. Curiouser and curiouser.

May carried in a platter of cheese, nuts, olives and fruit, which she placed on the low coffee table. Sparks sat forward to assemble a small plate of carefully chosen nibbly bits, then handed it to Fletcher. He tucked a blanket around Fletcher's knees and placed his drink within arm's reach on the end table. Sparks took his nursing duties very seriously. Once everyone was settled with drinks and snacks, May was ready to begin.

'I heard from Jean,' May said. 'She's taken the whole family to Cornwall for a few days. Hopefully that will be enough to protect them. I told her not to take anything edible from home and to throw out anything that could've been tampered with. I'm not sure what else can be done.'

'Is her daughter doing the same in their house?' Fletcher asked, as he chose his next tasty morsel. 'I can't stop thinking about Juan's coffee pods. So devious.'

May nodded.

'David says he doesn't think he sent those messages to me last night,' Fletcher continued. 'He'd had a lot to drink, so he couldn't be certain, but he doesn't remember sending them.'

'I had a look at the texts,' Bastian said. 'They do seem to have come from David's phone. Who else would have access to it?'

'The vicarage was full of people coming and going yesterday,' May replied. 'Once the news was out, the parish kicked into high gear, bringing meals and popping in to see how he was doing, or trying to find out the latest news. Did anyone stay with David into the evening?'

Fletcher shook his head. 'That's just it. David says he saw off the last well-wisher by eight. The texts weren't sent until just after nine. He was alone by then with the phone charging on the sideboard.'

'It's possible the texts were written earlier and scheduled to be sent at that time,' Bastian said. 'An app would be necessary to do that. I'd need to check David's phone to confirm it.'

'Or someone entered the house after David fell asleep,' May said.

A shiver ran up Fletcher's spine. How horrible to think of someone lurking around the room while one slept, oblivious to the danger.

'I've added the latest message to our list,' she said, as she handed copies to everyone. Minty took one but didn't look at it. She seemed preoccupied with other things.

Added to their previous list was the following:

<u>Fourth message:</u>

> It's a foolish father that doesn't know his own child. We all know little Clemmie isn't really yours. LK
> The Merchant of Venice, said by Lancelet Gobbo Act 2, Scene 2
> 'It is a wise father that knows his own child.'
> LK = Louis Kirkland? Now using first name, last name?

'Whoever is sending the texts,' May said, 'they're getting more personal. This one uses initials, as do all, apart from the second message, but this one also uses Clementine's nickname, making the Kirkland family the obvious target.'

'Unless we know of any other young Clemmie's in the area?' Fletcher said. He looked around as everyone, apart from Minty, shook their heads. Minty was staring off into space with a dreamy look on her face. Fletcher wondered briefly if she might be having a stroke. Then she shook her head and seemed her normal self again.

'Now that it seems the messages are focussed on the bookshop,' Bastian began, 'I've asked myself how they're being sent.'

Fletcher sensed that Bastian was about to launch into one of his technical lectures. He took a sip of his G&T and forced himself to concentrate. Sparks adjusted his position beside him.

'Does the sender have all of our contact details?' Bastian continued. 'That would suggest someone local, someone we all know.'

'But Fletcher didn't receive the first message, and neither of us received the third one. You forwarded it to me,' May replied. 'Are they picking and choosing who receives the messages each time?'

'I didn't receive any of them,' Sparks said.

'Exactly,' Bastian replied, standing up to refill his glass from the trolley, leaving out the vodka this time. 'There are different ways to message. We call them all text messages, but the way they work differs enormously. Nowadays, most people use apps, like WhatsApp. As long as the recipient has the same app, you've got unlimited messaging and usually the ability to video message too.

'An actual text message, called an SMS, uses the mobile network to send messages. The technology's been around since the nineties and almost every mobile uses SMS as its default messaging tool. It's a bit like making a textual phone call.'

He returned to his seat as he continued. 'There's also iMessaging, which can only be used between Apple devices. They look and act like SMS messages, but they use wifi or your phone's data network to send messages.' He paused to sip his drink.

'I first assumed these messages were being sent via SMS because it's not through an app and it's not just iPhones receiving them. But, if the sender had all of our contacts and was messaging using SMS, then it would be more likely the same people would receive the messages each time. That's not the case.'

'You received them all,' Fletcher said. 'What does that mean?'

'I think it means that I was in the right place each time. They seem to centre around the shop. With SMS or iMessage, the sender could be anywhere. Even the other side of the world,' Bastian explained. 'After the most recent text, I took a closer look and realised that the messages don't use either of those protocols. They're actually sent via Bluetooth in a way that some dating apps use. Or so I'm told.'

Sparks nodded. 'I dabbled with online dating at one time,' he said. 'I remember that feature.'

Fletcher raised his eyebrows. Sparks was full of surprises.

Minty had begun to gently snore in her chair.

'Bluetooth?' May said. 'That has quite a limited range, doesn't it?'

'Exactly,' Bastian replied.

Fletcher looked from one to the other of them. There was something he was missing. Though he was able to identify a forged Van Gogh from a few brushstrokes, much of technology remained beyond him.

'Bluetooth allows you to connect to anyone within a radius of about ten metres,' Bastian said. 'In a dating app it means you can see who might be interested in getting to know one better within a venue, like a bar or club. It's dependent on having both Bluetooth and location switched on, which most people do. The odd person who doesn't have those functions enabled wouldn't receive the messages, which explains the gaps in who received the texts in the shop.'

'So, the sender wouldn't need anyone's contact details? Just be near enough to connect via Bluetooth?' May asked.

Bastian nodded.

'Just a moment,' Fletcher said. 'Let me make sure I understand this.' He sat forward, holding the sling in place with his good hand, to look at Bastian. 'The messages aren't sent to individuals. It's more of a blanket text based on geographic location. Like throwing a bunch of balls in the air. Some people catch one, and some don't, but you have to be close enough to catch one in the first place?'

'That's one way of describing it,' Bastian said. 'Accurate enough for our purposes. The most important take away from this is that the person must be nearby when the texts are sent. This kind of messaging is all about proximity.' He set his empty glass on the table. 'Which means that when the messages are sent, the killer is *in the bookshop*.'

CHAPTER SEVENTEEN

SHE'S NOT THERE

F letcher leaned back against the sofa, his stomach churning. It was horrible to think of someone who wished him harm being in such comforting and familiar places as the vicarage and May's bookshop. He'd imagined a stranger, some mysterious troublemaker, coming to the village to cause havoc. That now seemed a thoroughly ridiculous idea. This person was close. It was someone they knew.

He tried to recall who was in the shop when the second message was sent.

'We should make a list of everyone we can remember being there at the time each message was received,' Fletcher said.

'I know it's only been a few days,' May replied, 'but I'm certain my list won't be very accurate. I wasn't paying much attention to the customers the first time and I was scanning the room for fingers on the send button, not really noticing faces the next time. Still, it's a decent idea. Let's give it a shot.'

She collected pens and paper from her desk at the window and she, Fletcher and Bastian set to work while Sparks refreshed their drinks and Minty continued to doze. Fifteen minutes later they compared their lists.

Bastian was the only one present for all three messages. His lists of names differed from May's and Fletcher's.

'Was Geoffrey there for the first message?' Bastian asked. 'I don't think he was.'

'I'm sure he was looking at a cookbook.' May looked at her piece of paper. 'Perhaps I'm thinking of the second message. Oh dear, this seems pointless.'

'Not completely pointless,' Bastian said. 'A few of the same people do appear in all of our recollections. Geoffrey, Betty and Jean in particular. None of them seem likely, but I guess you never really know.' He shrugged. 'I'll keep these. They may come in handy.'

'How strange to think it's someone we all know,' Sparks said. 'It's hard to imagine any of the people I know in Blackheath doing such a thing.'

'I suppose we never really know what goes on behind closed doors,' May said.

'The word is definitely out about these texts,' Bastian added. 'The shop was full again this morning. If it continues and the crowd grows, it'll make it even harder to identify who's sending them.'

'I think it's time to call it a night,' Sparks said, giving Fletcher a worried look. 'This young chap needs his rest.'

Fletcher smiled gratefully, exhausted by recent events. His shoulder had started to throb, signalling that it was probably time for another dose of painkillers.

Bastian and Sparks gathered their things. May and Fletcher walked them to the door to say goodnight.

'How are you, Bastian? Any news?' Fletcher couldn't resist, even though May was giving him the evil eye.

Bastian stopped and turned to Fletcher, looking mildly confused. 'Not really,' he said. 'I've got an estate sale next week that seems promising. A comic-book collector. I'm thinking of setting up a shelf for comics in the shop. Seems to be an area we've overlooked.'

'That sounds fascinating,' Fletcher said. 'Nothing else going on? In your life, for example?' May had ceased trying to stop Fletcher's questioning and was waiting for Bastian's answer with rapt attention.

Bastian looked from Fletcher to May and back again. 'No,' he said. 'Nothing in particular.'

'Just thought I'd ask,' Fletcher replied. 'Haven't had a proper chat for a while.'

Bastian said his goodnights and left looking bemused.

'What the hell was that all about?' Sparks asked as soon as Bastian was out of earshot.

'Fletch, you're looking awfully peaky. We should get you straight to bed,' May said.

Fletcher did his best to look unwell.

Sparks smiled at them, then shook his head. 'Thick as thieves,' he said as he waved goodbye. 'Thick as thieves.'

Minty stretched in the armchair. 'I think we could all do with a hot drink,' she said. 'I'll make the Horlicks.' She toddled off to the kitchen, humming a tune. At least Minty was in a good mood.

Fletcher couldn't help but wonder why.

CHAPTER EIGHTEEN

GET IT ON

May woke up to see a small, toothless child standing beside her bed. The odd little person stretched out a claw-like hand. May screamed and shrank away.

'May! For God'th thake. Thop thcreaming. I need your helpth,' Minty lisped.

May clutched at her pounding heart. 'Minty. Christ almighty, you almost gave me a heart attack. What's happened? I can barely understand you without your teeth.'

'There'th been an unforthunate inthident,' Minty said. 'You need thoo come with me.'

May threw back the duvet and sat up. She felt groggy and slightly dizzy. What could've happened? 'Are you all right?' She looked her mother over. Minty seemed fine. She was wearing a filmy peignoir over a black silk chemise. 'What on earth are you wearing?' The outfit was a departure from her usual wool flannel nightgowns.

'Never mind that. Justh come with me.' She pulled at May's arm.

May stood. The room tilted. She sat down again. 'I don't feel very well.' She rubbed at her head. 'How much did I drink last night?'

Minty cleared her throat. 'I may have put a little thomething in your Horlickth,' she said. 'Jutht to help you thleep.'

May raised her head. 'You did what?'

'I needed thome privacy this evening.' Minty shrugged. 'It'll wear off thoon enough. Now come.' She tugged at May's arm again.

Un-bloody-believable. Drugged by her own mother.

May stood, more carefully this time. The room remained stationary. 'You're never making the Horlicks again,' she grumbled, then slowly followed Minty downstairs to her bedroom in the converted sitting room.

In the dim light of the bedside lamp, May was surprised to see a naked man lying in Minty's bed. On closer inspection, she recognised the man as Humphrey Oslac, the son of her drama teacher at Blackheath High. He was lying ominously still, eyes staring, with a grin frozen on his face and what appeared to be an enormous erection creating a pup tent under the sheet. May stepped back into the entry hall, pulling Minty with her.

'Is that... did you... how in the world... is he?' She stopped to catch her breath. 'I don't know where to begin,' May said.

'I told you we bumpthed into each other in the village,' Minty said. 'Apparently, he alwayth fanthied me. One thing led to another and... You muthn't deny me a few little pleathures.'

'Go put your teeth in. I can't have this discussion with you lisping and spitting at me,' May said. 'Why did you take your teeth out in the first place? Actually, don't answer that. Just go put them back in.'

'We decithed to have a little thleep between thessions and you know I can't thleep with my teeth in,' Minty said.

'Everything all right down there?' Fletcher stage-whispered from the top of the stairs.

'No, it is not,' May said. 'We have a problem. A big one.'

Fletcher crept down the stairs, his right arm in its sling, his left gripping the handrail. 'How much did we drink last night?'

May gave Minty a hard look. 'You didn't. Not Fletch too? He's injured!'

Minty shrugged, eyes wide with false innocence.

Fletcher made his way over to them and peeked into Minty's bedroom. 'Oh, I say. Hello there.' He paused. 'Isn't that... Is he... Is that what I think it is?' He looked at Minty with something almost resembling respect. 'How on earth?'

'Yes, yes,' Minty said, sounding much more composed once her dentures were in place. 'It's all very shocking. A woman of my age, blah-blah-blah. The question is, what are we going to *do* with him?'

'What do you mean?' Fletcher replied. 'I'll ring 999. They'll come and deal with him. Unless...' He looked at May with dawning concern.

'No.' She shook her head. 'This is all Minty.' They looked at the tiny woman standing in the doorway, adjusting her wig.

Aware of the attention, Minty stood tall and raised her chin. 'It was all going swimmingly. We'd had a lovely time and were going to have a little sleep, then he just sort of froze and made a gurgling sound. I thought at first perhaps he was having an org–'

'Yes, all right! Spare us the details,' May said. She looked again at the grinning body in the bed. 'Sounds like a heart attack, but it doesn't explain that.' She pointed at the protruding sheet. 'Did he take anything? Before you...' She gestured to her mother and Humphrey, feeling nauseated.

'He did take a handful of little blue pills. Said it would guarantee a good evening and I must say, I had nothing to complain about.' Minty clutched the peignoir to her chest. 'I haven't had a night like that since–'

May held up one hand. 'I'm begging you. Only the bare facts, please.'

'Bare facts indeed,' Fletcher said, raising one eyebrow. He and Minty snorted, then pulled themselves together under May's scowl.

May took a deep breath and let it out slowly. Losing her temper would only make things worse. 'Why can't we ring 999?'

'It's Mildred Oslac's son!' Minty said. 'He's married to that nice Muriel from your class at the high school. Imagine the gossip. The village would be buzzing with it. Muriel would be devastated and I'd be labelled a wanton hussy.'

'You *are* a wanton hussy,' May said, reaching the limits of her patience.

'Polly May, how dare you!'

'The evidence is almost poking us in the face.' May pointed at the body, still grinning gormlessly from the pillows.

Fletcher looked at Humphrey Oslac. 'Let's not forget Humphrey's involvement here. He's the married party. HO by name, ho by nature.' He laughed at his own joke, then realised the women weren't listening to him at all.

'After everything I've done for you, this is how–' Minty was stomping one foot, her hands in fists.

'Everything you've done for *me*?!' May was almost shouting. 'You wouldn't even hold my hand when we crossed the road. Half the time you had no idea where I was or what I was doing.'

'I wanted for you to be *independent*,' Minty said. 'Is that so wrong?'

'At five years old, a child needs to hold her mother's hand. Even the most negligent parent knows that.' May's cheeks were pink with emotion. 'And don't think I haven't noticed that your hip is obviously *fine*!'

'Ladies! Please!' Fletcher stepped between them, raising his good arm in an appeasing gesture. 'Let's deal with the problem at hand. Something has to be done with him. Immediately, if not sooner.'

Both women were panting with rage but managed to calm themselves. May waggled her head slowly from side to side, stretching the tight muscles in her neck. 'Fine,' she said. 'What are you suggesting?' May looked at Minty. 'That we dispose of the body?'

'No.' Minty shook her head. 'Nothing like that. The family needs to be able to mourn properly. Just move him somewhere else.' She made fluttery gestures with her hands, as if moving a dead body was as easy as dusting the bookshelves.

May closed her eyes for one long breath before speaking. 'I suppose we can dress him and sit him in the TV room. There's no impropriety in visiting old friends.'

'No, no.' Minty wasn't satisfied. 'He needs to be out of the house.'

'In the garden?' Fletcher said, confused.

'No, away from here,' Minty replied. 'Imagine the old biddies at the church talking about him dying here in the middle of the night. They'll assume he was May's lover.' She looked at May. 'Unless you don't mind that, dear?'

May didn't much care what anyone thought of her, but the idea that she'd been shagging Humphrey Oslac was not an appealing one. Though still relatively handsome, years spent driving a bus had softened his once-firm waist and widened his arse. In contrast, his mind had narrowed over the years until he'd become an unrelenting bore. The notion that she would choose to spend time with Humphrey Oslac, much less be intimate with the man, was revolting. May's distaste must've been evident on her face because Minty turned back to Fletcher.

'*Away from here*,' she said with decision.

'But how?' Fletcher said. 'Could we put him in the boot of

the Land Rover and take him somewhere?'

'The caves,' Minty said. She looked across the room to the wheelchair she'd insisted on bringing home from the hospital. 'You can take him through the caves and leave him in the church. We'll dress him, put him in the chair. The cellar will be a challenge, but I don't think he'll mind bumping down the stairs.'

May sighed in exasperation but started to collect discarded clothing from the floor.

Fletcher wasn't quite there yet. 'Caves? What caves?'

'The Blackheath caves,' Minty explained. 'The tunnels run for miles under the heath, even down to the river. May used to play in them as a child, knows them like the back of her hand.'

'More of Minty's responsible parenting,' May said, fishing a pair of boxers out from under the bed and wishing she had a set of Sparks's laundry tongs. 'The caverns were made by ancient chalk miners. It's a wonder I didn't get lost and die down there.' She stood up and swiped her hair away from her face. 'This house used to be a brothel. There's a tunnel that runs from the cellar to the crypt of the church. Make of that what you will.'

The crypt of St Julian's had been renovated a few years before to create a space for the children's Bible school and other events. In place of the bodies, there were three carpeted event rooms, a storage room, a large utility room and an IKEA kitchen. It had been a very popular addition to the church.

May walked over to the bed and carefully pulled back the sheet, revealing Humphrey in all his glory. 'Minty! Why on earth is he wearing a condom?!'

Fletcher bellowed with laughter. He moved away from the bed to sit down on a chair and compose himself.

'I don't know where he's been,' Minty said with distaste. 'You can never be too careful. I hope you insist on all of your lovers wearing protection, Polly May.'

May decided to ignore this comment. She looked at the offending appendage in frustration. 'Well, we can't leave it on him. One of us has to remove it.'

May and Minty both looked at Fletcher who was still chuckling in the corner, gently cradling his arm. He stopped abruptly. 'Oh, no. No, no *no*. Not in a million years. I am *not* doing it. There is no way on God's green earth you can make me remove a condom from a cadaver. Absolutely not. Besides, I'm injured!'

Eventually, wearing a Marigold washing-up glove on his good hand and with the use of a pair of tweezers, Fletcher managed to remove and dispose of the condom. He chucked the glove and tweezers in the bin along with it.

'Go boil your hand,' May said. 'We'll get him dressed.'

As she threaded Humphrey's foot into his trouser leg, May blanched at the smell of him. It wasn't the scent of death, too early for that, it was the horrible old man smell that she hated. That greasy, grassy odour so redolent of care homes. May had a very sensitive sense of smell. When she'd noticed her own body odour changing after menopause, she'd done some research (of course she had) and found that there was a certain compound called *nonenal* that was prevalent on the skin of older human beings. It was the aroma of human cells decaying. Yes, really.

The scent reminded her vividly of Fletcher's father, a small, angry man who'd proudly declared that he'd never needed to wear deodorant since he produced no body odour. The entire Redmond home reeked of Fletcher Senior's BO.

That old man smell was one of the reasons May thought she would probably never have sex again. Unless she could find a young toyboy, but that really wasn't a very appealing prospect.

Getting Humphrey's trousers zipped was becoming an ordeal with the stubborn erection remaining bolt upright. Finally, Minty grasped his penis and pressed it down while May jerked the zip upwards, as Fletcher crossed his legs and winced in the corner.

Once Humphrey was fully dressed, May and Fletcher prepared themselves for the next phase of their plan. May instructed Fletcher to put on something dark with sturdy shoes. She went to her bedroom and dressed herself similarly. Back in Minty's room, the three of them manoeuvred Humphrey into the wheelchair and pushed him to the top of the cellar steps.

'I think this will be the most difficult part,' May said. 'Fletch, I'll go in front and we can bump him down the steps one by one. We don't want to jiggle the body enough to leave any marks. It won't be easy with your arm in a sling, but if we just take our time and ease the chair over each step, it'll be fine.'

Before May could move into position, Minty stepped forward and gave the wheelchair a hard shove. It careened down the stairs with Humphrey jerking back and forth in the seat before spilling him onto the stone floor below.

May and Fletcher, both temporarily speechless, looked at Minty.

'Not so difficult after all,' Minty said.

'He'll be covered in post-mortem bruises,' May replied. 'How's that going to look?'

'A little mystery for the boys in blue.' Minty shrugged. 'They love that sort of thing.' She pulled her peignoir tighter. 'I'll leave the rest of it to you two. I'm knackered. Ta-ra.'

With that, she turned and headed back towards her bedroom.

'Are you sure you don't want to kill her?' Fletcher asked. 'A quick shove at the top of the stairs? A drop of rat poison in her tea?'

'It's remarkably tempting,' May replied, then turned back to look at the corpse lying in her cellar. 'But I can only deal with one body at a time.'

CHAPTER NINETEEN

SUBTERRANEAN HOMESICK BLUES

Down in the cellar, they lifted Humphrey back into the wheelchair with Fletcher helping as much as he could one-handed. 'Just keep hold of his head,' May said, heaving his body into the chair. 'Christ, it's always the head that gets in the way.'

Once he was settled into place, she went to scour the cellar shelves.

'We need a torch and some string,' May mumbled, sifting through boxes.

Fletcher looked around the enormous subterranean space. It had been damp-proofed and carpeted years before, creating a large, open-plan room. The walls were whitewashed stone, the carpet a speckled blue, with fluorescent lights overhead. He'd been down there only a handful of times before. May would often disappear to the cellar to work on one project or another. She had a small lab at the end towards the front of the house with a computer and two monitors. This is where she conducted any necessary online research on the rare occasion that her library failed her.

At the opposite end was an oversized flat-screen television, a leather sectional sofa and an American-style fridge freezer. That was James's Sofa of Shame, as May called it. It's where he would watch football and box sets of *Only Fools and Horses* and *Noel's House Party*.

'What are you going to do with all that?' he asked, nodding towards the opposite end of the room.

May looked up from her rummaging. 'Charity, maybe. I dread trying to get it out of here though. It was a bugger getting that fridge down the steps.' She held up a large torch and two reels of garden twine. 'This should do us.' She moved towards the bookcases on the other side of her lab. 'I might need some help with this,' she said. 'It hasn't been opened in decades.' May grabbed the edge of a bookcase and heaved. Nothing happened.

Fletcher joined her, placing his free hand beside hers. 'On three,' he said. 'One, two, three...'

The bookcase began to scrape across the stone floor, concealed metal wheels screeching in protest, setting Fletcher's teeth on edge. A waft of musty, dry air escaped, smelling of earth and cold. As soon as the opening was wide enough to accommodate the wheelchair, they stopped, coughing and fanning chalk dust away from their faces. Fletcher looked into the hole behind the bookcase. A narrow, ink-black corridor crawled into oblivion with a pale cloud of particles hanging in the dank air. 'We're going in there?' he asked.

May nodded. 'It's not so bad once you're deeper inside. The first ten metres or so are the worst.' She switched on the torch, shining its beam into the murk. Fletcher drew back, his skin crawling at the thought of entering that seemingly endless abyss. He'd never believed in monsters, but if they did exist, they lived in the Blackheath caves.

'You played in these tunnels as a *child*?' he said.

May nodded. 'Hide-and-seek, pirate treasure hunting. There was a time when I didn't need the twine to find my way out again.' She looped one end of a skein around a large hook beside the doorway. 'But that was a long time ago. We won't take any chances tonight.' She stepped into the darkness and began to uncoil the string.

'I found a skeleton in here once.' Her voice sounded distant, muted, swallowed up by the thick walls of the tunnel. 'Probably a vagrant who wandered in from the river end. The rats had almost picked him clean.'

'You had a very strange childhood,' Fletcher said, remaining on the threshold.

'No shit, Sherlock,' May replied as she brushed past him coming out of the tunnel, then gestured for Fletcher to enter. 'Ladies first,' she said. 'Come on then, you carry the torch in front. I'll push Muggins here behind you.'

Fletcher swallowed. He glanced into the cellar behind them, which seemed warm and welcoming, comforting in its normality compared to the gloomy passage he was about to enter. May was waiting, tapping one foot with impatience. He stepped forward, holding his injured arm closer while wielding the torchlight like a sword with his good one. The wheelchair bumped into his heel.

'Ouch!' he said. Bending to rub his ankle, he almost banged his head on the chalk wall.

'Come on,' May said. 'We haven't got all night. Mordecai opens the church at sunrise.'

Fletcher walked on. The wheelchair bumped along the rough, uneven ground behind him, occasionally scraping the wall on one side. The grating sound of metal on stone did nothing to improve his mood.

'It opens up just ahead,' May said.

Fletcher thought they'd been walking in a straight line on a gentle descent, but it was difficult to tell. The walls were close, covered in carvings of names and dates. Under different circumstances, he would've enjoyed stopping to read them. His eye caught the year 1780, then further along, a name scratched out in a childish hand, Castor Morrigan.

The air grew cooler as they progressed, then suddenly the walls seemed to fall away as they entered a large cavern. May took the torch and searched the darkness, revealing chains, shackles and a long iron table against one wall.

'Good Lord, was this place used as a torture chamber?' Fletcher asked.

May shook her head. 'As far as I can tell, they date from the time of the brothel, which seemed to cater for all tastes.' She continued to look around. The light revealed a round room with rough pointed archways opening in various directions. The white chalk walls were decorated with drawings here and there. Fletcher spotted a bear on its hind legs, a crocodile, and a horse. The images were too cartoonish to be ancient. Fletcher had been to Lascaux. He knew Palaeolithic art when he saw it. The Blackheath caves were decorated in what he guessed to be eighteenth-century graffiti.

'What an extraordinary place,' he said. 'I'm surprised it hasn't been turned into a tourist attraction.'

May was playing the beam back and forth between two openings, each of them guarded by a cartoon soldier in bearskin and red coat. 'There's another section of caves at the end of one of these tunnels. Minty used to go to dances there. They tried to make money from it at one time. I believe it was very successful until a visitor died. Something about noxious fumes, lack of ventilation. I forget.' She shook her head, dismissing the conversation. The torch landed on the right-hand tunnel. 'We'll go this way,' she said. 'It's the long way, but I don't think you're ready for the bones.' May headed for the archway, taking Humphrey and the torch with her.

'Noxious fumes? Bones!?' Fletcher replied, hastening to

catch up before he was left alone in the darkness. He'd almost preferred the narrow corridor, where at least he could see what was to his left and right. Here, it was black on all sides. Anything could be lurking out there, extending a withered hand to grab an ankle or brush against a cheek. He could step into a deep hole, never seeing it in the absolute obsidian darkness. And who would ever find him? Fletcher hurried on, trying to breathe as shallowly as possible.

The ground continued to descend for a time, then almost imperceptibly, they started to climb. Fletcher was just about to reach the end of his patience when the wide tunnel they'd entered became another narrow corridor, ending in a heavy wooden door.

'I'll need your help again,' May said, tugging at the iron ring on the door.

Fletcher squeezed past the wheelchair, his back rubbing against the chalk walls as he clambered around the wheels.

'Why did I wear cashmere?' he said, brushing at the arm of his jumper.

'Treat yourself to a new one once this is all over,' May replied. 'Now, come on and heave-ho.'

It took them a few tries before the door opened to reveal a solid wall of stone.

'Christ on a bike,' Fletcher said. 'Now what do we do?'

'This is the easy part,' May replied, reaching up to release a small catch then sliding the stone effortlessly to one side. The interior of the church's utility room was revealed with its deep sink, stacks of extra chairs, and rows of shelves holding cleaning products, loo roll, boxes of tea bags, cartons of UHT milk, tins of biscuits, sturdy cups and saucers, lightly stained tea towels and slightly chipped dinner plates.

'How was the entrance to the tunnels not found and sealed up in the crypt renovations?' Fletcher asked.

May rolled her eyes. 'Who do you think organised the renovations?' She had been a very active member of the planning committee.

'Thank fuck for that,' Fletcher said. 'Let's dump Humphrey and go home. I need a cup of tea, then a tot of whisky. Then another cup of tea. And maybe some cake.'

May nodded in agreement, then raised her head to listen. 'Do you hear that?'

The sound of someone whistling was growing steadily louder.

'It must be Mordecai,' May said. 'What's he doing here at this hour?' They backtracked into the tunnel the way they'd come, shoving Humphrey and the wheelchair ahead of them. May slid the stone wall into place just as the utility room door opened and Mordecai Page entered, whistling the theme tune to *Some Mothers Do 'Ave 'Em.*

May and Fletcher, ears pressed to the wall, heard a chair being scraped across the floor then the sound of a biscuit tin being opened, followed by rustling and chomping. Fletcher thought of Mordecai's always filthy hands and made a mental note to never again partake of the biscuits offered at church events.

They listened as boxes were shuffled around on the metal shelves, the chair squeaked, then silence, punctuated by the occasional sound of rustling paper.

'What's he doing in there?' Fletcher whispered. 'Reading?'

May squinted in concentration then her face puckered in disgust. 'Do you remember what David said Mordecai hides in the utility cupboard?'

'Dear God, no.' Fletcher recoiled, as bile rose in the back of his throat. 'Surely not. Not *in the church?!*'

Mordecai grunted, then produced a phlegmy cough and farted lavishly. Fletcher gagged on the other side of the wall.

The biscuit tin banged again, then more crunching and crinkling could be heard.

'It sounds like he's having a pornographic picnic in there,' Fletcher said.

May reached up to the catch above the door. 'I'll sort him out,' she whispered.

Fletcher grabbed her arm. 'No! What are you doing?' he hissed.

May motioned for them to step away from the wall. They pushed Humphrey deeper into the tunnel, so they could have a proper conversation.

'Who knows how long he's going to be in there tickling the ivories,' May said. 'We don't have all night. We need to dump Humphrey and get out before anyone else arrives. I'll deal with Mordecai, then we can get this shit sorted and go home.'

'That doesn't make sense,' Fletcher said.

'I don't know what else we're supposed to do,' May replied.

'No.' Fletcher shook his head. 'The plural. It doesn't work. Why would it be plural?'

May gave him a blank stare. 'I beg your pardon.'

'The ivories,' he clarified. 'Tickling the ivories. It shouldn't be plural.'

May rolled her eyes. 'I don't know exactly what he's doing in there, nor do I want to know. The plural may well be valid.'

Fletcher shook his head again. 'Not in common usage,' he said. 'It would be something more like "pulling the pud" or "choking the chicken", both singular, you see. Or "burping the worm" works too. "Conducting the one-handed concerto" has a certain elegance to it. Since we're in a church "banging the bishop" seems particularly apt. Or "punishing the Pope", though this isn't a Catholic establishment.' He tilted his head as he pondered. 'Interesting how consonance is so often used in the English idioms. Not the same in other languages. The Germans say *die Möhre schrubben*, to scrub one's carrot. In Russia it's *lysogo v kulake gonyat*, to pet one's monkey.' Fletcher laughed softly to himself. 'The Victorians just called it self-abuse, which is a pretty clear indicator of the general Victorian view of sex and pleasure. I've always liked the Cockney use of "J Arthur". It's succinct and discreet, not too overt for mixed company.'

May stared at Fletcher. She blinked once. Twice. Then, before Fletcher could react, she moved to the sliding wall and was gone.

CHAPTER TWENTY

MY DING-A-LING

Fletcher crouched in the darkness; ear once again pressed to the wall. He heard May shout, then Mordecai's scream, a crashing sound, a resounding thud, then silence.

Fletcher dithered. He gripped the wheelchair, almost comforted by Humphrey's silent presence. 'Fuck this,' he said before fumbling for the catch above the door. In his distress, he couldn't get the damn thing to work. Banging on the wall, he shouted, 'May! May! Are you all right? MAY!'

At last, the wall slid slowly back and May was revealed, looking composed and bemused by his agitation. 'Calm down,' she said. 'The problem sorted itself. It's not pretty, but it works for us. Come on and bring Humphrey.'

Fletcher stumbled into the utility room, pulling the wheelchair awkwardly forward with his good hand, relieved to be out of the tunnels and back to civilisation. He recoiled when he saw Mordecai Page's body sprawled on the cupboard floor, one hand still gripping his manhood, a copy of *Mayfair* magazine beside him open to an article entitled *Cotswold Kay: Our Fergie Lookalike.*

'That must be a collector's item,' Fletcher said, focussing on the vintage magazine, trying very hard not to look directly at the gurning man on the floor beside it. He took one quick peek to see if Minty's impressive description of Mordecai's willy was correct. Fletcher had seen better.

'I'm not touching the thing,' May said as she washed her hands at the utility sink. 'That magazine could be worth a million pounds and I'd still leave it where it lies.' She shook her head. 'That was extremely unpleasant to witness, but it's solved our problem.' She nodded at the body on the floor. 'I stepped through the wall, shouted "boo" and Mordecai screamed then keeled right over. I suppose he *was* in his nineties, and he probably already had an elevated heart rate due to his... activity.' She made a face of disgust. 'I feel the need to wash my eyeballs.' She splashed her face with water.

Fletcher rubbed his forehead and swallowed. 'I'm fairly certain I've got a raging nervous breakdown brewing just below the surface,' he said. 'At the moment, I'm far too tired to deal with that on top of everything else. Shall we address Body Number One now? We can circle back to Mordecai afterwards.'

May looked at the crusty hand towel beside the sink, then dried her hands on her trousers before rubbing her face. 'I think this little spectacle tells the story quite succinctly,' she said, gesturing to Mordecai. 'Humphrey is a bigger challenge. If we prop him up on a pew in the nave, it could look like he came to the church for some reason, then had a heart attack.' She took charge of the wheelchair and opened the door into the main part of the crypt.

Fletcher looked from one body to the other and tried to pull himself together. 'Humphrey must be covered in bruises from the fall down the cellar steps,' he said. 'And I'm sure they have some way of telling he's recently had sex. Minty's DNA must be all over him. I hope to God she doesn't have a criminal record.' He looked at May. 'Does she? I wouldn't put it past her.'

May shrugged. It was possible, but most likely any crimes Minty had committed were well before DNA was collected.

'An innocent heart attack isn't going to explain this abominable situation,' Fletcher said. 'Two dead bodies on the same morning! People will assume they're linked. It's too much of a coincidence.'

Standing in the church utility cupboard, gripping the handles of the wheelchair that held the body of her mother's dead lover while the church caretaker lay at her feet gripping his John Thomas, May turned very slowly until she was looking directly at Fletcher. 'It may surprise you to know that I don't have all the answers, Dr Redmond. If *you* have any bright ideas, do share them. I'm all ears.'

Fletcher took a step back, opened his mouth, then shut it again. He shook his head. 'No, you're right. Putting him on a pew makes perfect sense. It'll be fine.'

May squinted.

'More than fine,' Fletcher hurried on. 'It's a brilliant idea. The most bloody brilliant idea in the whole history of bloody brilliant ideas.'

May shook her head with a look of irritation, but Fletcher could see that she was trying not to smile. 'I'm glad we're in agreement,' she replied. 'Now, let's get this fucker sorted.'

CHAPTER TWENTY-ONE

BRIDGE OVER TROUBLED WATER

May felt utterly exhausted. She'd not had more than a few hours' sleep in the previous two days, first because of the attack on Fletcher, then Minty's shenanigans. They'd propped Humphrey up on a pew at the back of the church. Fletcher placed a hymn book beside him to create a sense of realism. May couldn't resist opening it to 'Great is Thy Faithfulness' before leaving it beside the dead adulterer. She poured herself another cup of strong coffee from the moka pot. She'd wait until ten and see if there was another message. Then, she'd rest.

Sitting at the kitchen table, she closed her eyes and tried to absorb the peace. Fletcher was fast asleep in his room. He'd taken some painkillers as soon as they returned and conked right out. Minty had been up early and taken Bess and George for a 'walk'. This involved strolling to the bench on the heath in front of the house, where Minty would sit, striking up conversations with anyone who came within range. The dogs certainly didn't mind.

Greenway was the calmest it had been in days. The silence was intoxicating.

May jerked awake with a snort just before her head hit the pine kitchen table. Sitting still was not a good idea. She checked the time, two hours to go. A shower would probably be wise. She tentatively sniffed an armpit. The shower could wait. Washing then drying, undressing then redressing, it all felt like too much effort.

Hauling herself to standing, she bounced up and down on the balls of her feet for a moment to get the blood moving. A walk around the village and some food, that's what was needed.

In the hall, she picked up the post and spent a good five minutes searching for the dog leads before remembering they'd gone out with Minty. 'I need to pull myself together,' she muttered as she opened the door and set off.

On the other side of the heath, she could see a police car and the mortuary van outside the church. So, they'd found at least one of the bodies. May turned to give Minty a warning glare as she passed her bench, shaking her head to say, 'Don't even think about going to the church.' Minty just rolled her eyes and continued her conversation with a dog walker whose cockapoo was making friends with Bess and George.

May carried on into the village. She had a chat with the ladies at the chemist, made a few purchases there and bought some prawns from the fishmonger. Eventually she found a seat in the window of a café where she settled with a large cappuccino and a ham and cheese toastie, nodding hello to friends when they passed. It was impossible to be in Blackheath without seeing someone she knew.

Removing the post from her handbag, she sifted through the bills and flyers as she ate. There was a time when May's post would have been full of letters and cards from friends near and far. Now it was all text messages and emails, maybe the occasional snapshot sent to her mobile. Even phone calls had become a rarity. No more familiar voices chatting in one's ear, just the same cold font tapped out in the shortest sentences possible. No rush of excitement at spotting familiar handwriting on an envelope that was sent to *you*, rather than a trite post on social media suitably edited for the world to see. No more holding the same piece of paper a friend had held while writing to you, seeing the coffee ring in the corner where they'd rested their cup, or words smeared by tears when the news was upsetting. Though technology seemed to be making the world smaller, May often felt that people were growing further apart.

Amongst all the bumpf was an official-looking envelope. Not a bill. Not a flyer. She opened it and began to read. Her stomach dropped. She thought she might be sick.

'May! Did you hear the news?' Darcy Cooper had plopped herself in the chair across from May. 'Humphrey Oslac *and* Mordecai Page were found in the church this morning. Both dead from heart attacks.'

'How dreadful,' May replied, refolding the letter and tucking it away.

'Humphrey had a bad heart for years,' Darcy continued. 'It was just a matter of time. Muriel thinks Humphrey knew he was dying and went to the church to be nearer to God.'

'Was he very devout?' May sipped coffee to hide her smile. Extraordinary, the mental gymnastics some people will do in order to avoid a painful truth.

'Such a shock for the family,' Darcy said, seeming to dodge the question. 'Thankfully, he had a good pension from the buses, so Muriel will be fine. She's got the flower shop to keep her busy, but she says she needs to get away to grieve properly, poor thing. Magaluf, most likely. Too many memories here.'

May nodded. She didn't trust herself to speak.

Darcy looked around the café, then leaned closer. 'You don't want to know what Mordecai was doing when they found *him*.' She shook her head in distaste. 'And in the church utility cupboard, of all places. I did tell David what he'd been hiding in there and David did nothing about it.'

'I think David has other things on his mind at the moment,' May said.

'Oh, of course he does,' Darcy said, immediately regretting her words. 'I just meant... well, it's a shame. Two deaths in one morning.'

May nodded. This news would certainly keep the village gossips busy for weeks.

'How's Fletcher doing? He must be so distressed.' Darcy placed one hand on May's arm, making sympathetic eyes at her.

'He's fine,' May said, extracting herself from Darcy's bony grip. 'Resting at the moment. He'll have the stitches out in a week or so.'

'Oh, yes. The stabbing. Awful.' Darcy's eyes seemed to grow larger. 'I was talking about the article in the paper this morning. We've all become accustomed to Fletcher and Barb in the last few months. I'm so glad we live in a place that doesn't get all bent out of shape over–'

'What article?' May interrupted, remembering the journalist Fletcher had mentioned. She felt the adrenaline rush into her bloodstream, causing her hands to ache. The public revelation of Fletcher's double life could be a positive step forward, or a devastating nightmare. It all depended on the way it was presented in the media. May clenched and unclenched her hands under the table.

Darcy reached into the bulging Bag for Life she seemed to carry everywhere. After rifling through the apparent filing system within the bag, she extracted a newspaper. The headline made May's nightmare an instant reality:

ANOTHER MAN APPROPRIATING THE LIVES OF WOMEN

May scanned the article.

...using his male privilege to take money from the pockets of female writers... further silencing of female voices... making a mockery of feminine desire...

Shit. Shit. Shit.

And it was a national paper.

May stuffed the post back into her handbag, left Darcy at the table, and went straight to the newsagents. Mr Demirci nodded at the paper as he rang up her purchase. 'Give our love to Dr Redmond,' he said. He reached up to the shelf behind the counter and picked up a packet of chocolate bourbons. 'His favourites. On the house.' He placed the biscuits on top of the newspaper. May could've kissed him for his kindness.

On the way to the bookshop she texted Sparks who would soon be heading to Greenway to see Fletcher.

> Have you seen the National Observer? I'll be home by 10.30. Wait for me before you show Fletch.

His reply was swift and to the point.

> Roger that.

Burgos Books was packed again. There were even people standing around on the pavement outside the shop, phone in hand, waiting to see what would happen. May squeezed through the door, managing to catch Bastian's eye behind the counter. She held up the paper, to which he nodded solemnly, then gestured for her to meet him at the back of the shop.

Jilly was helping out with the hot drinks again. 'What a

118

carry on,' she said, placing an espresso in May's hand. 'You'd think the Good Lord himself was expected. Is this all for those silly mobile phone messages?'

'I think so,' May replied. She thanked Jilly for the coffee then moved past her, smiling hello to familiar faces. Bastian was over at the door to his flat waiting for May.

Once upstairs in the peace of his sitting room, May dared to open the newspaper to read the full article while Bastian waited on the sofa. The sounds of someone cooking came from Bastian's kitchen. A pan banged onto the hob, a blender whined.

'Sorry,' he said. 'My... friend is staying over. I'll just...' He disappeared into the kitchen.

The sound of cooking quietened down and was replaced with a whispered discussion that quickly grew heated.

May tried to concentrate on the article as the hissed argument behind the door continued. Trouble in paradise already? Oh dear.

Once she finished reading, she refolded the paper carefully then closed her eyes with a long exhale. The kitchen had gone silent.

Bastian returned, running his hands through his hair, red-faced.

'Apologies,' he said.

'I'm guessing you've read it?' May said, opening her eyes.

'Yep,' he replied, returning to his place on the sofa. He seemed relieved that May hadn't asked about the commotion in the kitchen.

She leaned forward, resting her arms on her knees, preparing her evaluation.

'It could be worse,' she said. 'They haven't used Fletcher's name. Yet. I'm guessing she's going to drag it out, get more than one headline from the story, so full exposure is probably on the way. Still, it means they most likely don't have any real proof, just conjecture.'

'Yes,' Bastian replied. 'But the court of public opinion doesn't need evidence to convict. Have you spoken to Fletcher yet?'

May shook her head. 'He'll take it hard. It's such an invasion of privacy to be outed like this. And the language! "Appropriation", "male privilege". Barb's publisher didn't even know she was a man for the first few years. They assumed Fletcher Redmond was her husband or agent. It was only when she'd won her first RITA and they couldn't understand why she refused to accept the award in person that Fletcher had to come clean. If this journalist knew him and Barb, she'd never write such nonsense.' Standing up, May went to look out the window. The view was a beautiful one, encompassing the heath, St Julian's church, Minty on her bench entertaining someone who had a number of dogs on leads. May noticed that Bess and George had retreated from the pack by settling next to Minty on the bench. Over on the other side of the heath sat May's lovely home, Greenway. She imagined Fletcher asleep in his upstairs room, oblivious to the storm breaking over his head.

On the other hand... maybe this would be a *good* thing. The timing was forced, but Fletcher had been more open about Barb in the village in the last few months. He was becoming more comfortable with other people knowing. Perhaps now was the time when he could start to live openly in whatever way he chose. The papers would be fighting to tell his side of the story. He would have a platform, a voice. It would be like ripping off the plaster all at once: painful, but quickly over.

May's phone pinged in her handbag as Bastian's phone vibrated on the table.

Ten am. She'd almost forgotten about the messages.

'Shall we see what our Shakespearian slayer has to say today?' Bastian said, picking up his phone.

May extracted hers from her bag, swiped to wake up the screen, then felt her knees go weak. She had something even more personal to worry about.

> Suspicion haunts the guilty mind. I know you killed your husband. Where is he now?

CHAPTER TWENTY-TWO

MY BOYFRIEND'S BACK

Fletcher opened his eyes to see Sparks sitting on an armchair beside his bed wearing a black-and-white-striped shirt and a black eye mask. At his feet was a bulging sack marked 'SWAG'.

Fletcher laughed himself awake. 'You absolute nutter,' he said, wiping tears from his cheeks. 'Am I dreaming?'

Sparks did his best to maintain a straight face, but his eyes danced behind the mask. 'I don't know what you're on about, mate.' He brandished a toy pistol. 'Stick 'em up.'

'You're completely mad,' Fletcher said.

Sparks grinned. 'One arse bandit, at your service, sir.'

Fletcher laughed until the pain in his shoulder made him stop. He pointed at the bag at Sparks's feet. 'And what's that?' he asked. 'A bag of arse?'

'I'm afraid not,' Sparks replied.

Fletcher sorted out his painkillers, still sniggering whenever he looked at Sparks. The previous night's exertions had certainly not helped his healing. Sparks pushed the mask up to his forehead and opened the swag bag. He extracted homemade croissants, a flask of coffee, and a flask of hot chocolate. 'I thought we could have mochas,' he said, as he prepared two steaming mugs.

Fletcher took a moment to enjoy Sparks's handsome profile. Whatever happened in the future, he felt incredibly fortunate to have spent time with such a wonderful person.

'Have you seen May?' Fletcher asked.

'No,' Sparks replied, busying himself with the drinks. 'Minty let me in. She seems to be in a jolly mood this morning.'

'I bet she is,' Fletcher murmured.

Sparks perched on the edge of the bed as Fletcher, leaning against a bank of pillows, ate pastries and drank his mocha. He sighed with satisfaction. 'I'm feeling so much better now.'

Sparks patted his knee through the duvet, but a worried look crossed his face.

'I really am feeling better,' Fletcher assured him. 'Is there something else? You look troubled.'

Sparks turned his face away. 'Was that the front door? Perhaps May's back. I'll just go check.' He stood up and abruptly left the room.

Fletcher's stomach clenched. Something was definitely wrong. He checked the time. Had there been another message? Had it been about Sparks this time?

Throwing off the duvet with gusto, then immediately regretting the exertion, Fletcher carefully stood and shuffled his dressing gown over his shoulders.

As he made his way slowly down the stairs, he saw May and Sparks speaking in low voices in the entry hall. They made an unusual pair with Sparks in his bandit gear. Fletcher paused to listen but couldn't quite make out what they were saying. Then the dogs spotted him and started whining at the bottom of the stairs. May and Sparks looked up. Fletcher caught a flash of guilt, before they both smiled. The smiles were the most disturbing thing of all.

'What in God's name is going on?' Fletcher said. 'Has someone else died?'

'Apparently,' May said carefully. 'Humphrey Oslac and Mordecai Page were both found dead in the church this morning. Heart attacks, unrelated it seems.'

'Ah. Oh,' Fletcher began, caught off guard. 'How dreadful. What an absolute travesty. How devastating.'

May, standing behind Sparks, shook her head and motioned for Fletcher to tone it down.

'Of course,' Fletcher said, changing course, 'I didn't really know either of them. I suppose we all have to go at some point.' He made his way to the bottom of the staircase. 'Is that what you two were whispering about? You look like you're up to something.'

May looked at Sparks. 'Don't look at me. I'm not the one robbing banks in my spare time.'

Sparks swiped the mask from his forehead. 'I'll just quickly change.' He kissed Fletcher on the cheek as he passed him on his way to Fletcher's room.

'Come on down,' May said. 'I'll put the kettle on.'

Fletcher followed her to the kitchen with trepidation. Something odd was in the air. Had May and Sparks started a relationship? Surely not.

Though there *had* been that incident with Vincent Kingsley when they were at Cambridge. May had seemed more amused than hurt when Vincent started sleeping with Fletcher too. Had she decided to finally take her revenge?

Fletcher sat at the kitchen table, preparing himself for the worst. Once Sparks joined them in his usual shirt and knitted waistcoat, May pushed a newspaper across the table. Fletcher read the headline with something akin to relief. 'Is that all?' he said, laughing at their shocked faces.

'All?' May echoed. 'We thought you'd be devastated. Are you really not bothered?'

Fletcher took a moment to read the whole article before responding. May and Sparks busied themselves making a pot of tea, disagreeing over the use of bags or loose tea, before settling on two separate pots. May felt strongly that the risk of leaves between one's teeth outweighed any flavour benefits from the use of loose tea.

Once everyone was settled back at the table, Fletcher was ready to deliver his verdict. 'It's a load of tosh.'

'Yes,' May said. 'We can agree on that. The question is how you want to handle it. I suspect this won't be the end of it.'

'The other papers will be fighting to get your side of the story,' Sparks chipped in. 'If you want to tell it.'

Fletcher sipped his tea and looked towards the window. A gentle breeze sprinkled blossom on the windowsill. 'I don't know what I want to do. This needs to sink in before I make any decisions.'

'Whatever you decide, we're both here for you,' Sparks said.

May nodded in agreement.

'I know you are,' Fletcher said with a smile. 'Now, what else has been happening? Was there another text this morning?'

May's smile immediately dropped. 'You don't need to think about that at the moment,' she said. 'Just focus on getting better and deciding how you want to handle this article. I'm sure your agent and publisher will both be in touch soon enough with their own opinions on what you should do.'

Odd response. What was she hiding?

'That's true,' he said. 'I think what I need right now is a bath. Do you mind helping me with this thing?' Fletcher gestured at the sling on his arm and looked at Sparks.

Sparks raised both eyebrows in a devilish fashion. 'I'd be delighted.'

Once upstairs, Sparks disappeared into the en suite to run a hot bath. Fletcher took the opportunity to text Bastian and ask him about that morning's message.

'Rose or lavender?' Sparks popped his head out of the en suite and held up two bottles of Taylor's bath oil, causing Fletcher to jump.

'You choose,' Fletcher replied, randomly opening a drawer and pretending to carefully select a pair of socks.

'Righto,' Sparks said.

Fletcher shoved the black socks in his hand back into the drawer, completely the wrong choice for the tan trousers he'd laid out on the bed. Sparks must've seen straight through that ruse. His phone pinged with the forwarded text.

> Suspicion haunts the guilty mind. I know you killed your husband. Where is he now?

Fletcher inhaled sharply. 'I knew it!' he said.

CHAPTER TWENTY-THREE

STRAIGHTEN UP AND FLY RIGHT

Minty hummed 'In the Mood' as she made tea and toast for her late breakfast. She gave a little shimmy and a step-ball-change on her way to the fridge for the butter. After all the drama of the night before, she'd slept surprisingly well. Must've been all those lovely endorphins. She felt awful for Humphrey's family, but was glad that at least he'd died with a smile on his face.

Minty had seen May only in passing on the heath, and had seen neither hide nor hair of Fletcher, but assumed that everything had been dealt with. The police and the mortuary van had left the church without fuss. May had always been the most competent child.

Fletcher's new love had come to visit, such a nice man, and they'd had a pleasant chat about the dreaded National Loaf, the bread the government provided after the war. Minty told him how she would sieve the awful National Flour through a pair of old stockings to produce just enough white flour to make a decent loaf at home.

Before going upstairs to see Fletcher, Sparks gave each of

the dogs a new bone. They scurried off to opposite corners of the kitchen to enjoy their treasures in peace.

Minty sat at the kitchen table and sighed with pleasure. As she sipped tea and nibbled toast, her thoughts turned to the previous evening, before all the dying started. It really had been most gratifying and unexpected. 'You've still got it, ducky,' she said to herself.

Catching sight of the clock, Minty shook off the memories and hurried to finish her breakfast. Betty was coming round for a chat at any moment.

'The whole village is talking about it,' Betty said. 'Two deaths in the church this morning. It's very strange. Both of them had heart attacks, but the deaths don't seem to be related.'

'Mordecai Page was in the utility cupboard?' Minty asked, knowing very well that's where the entrance to the tunnels was situated. She would have to get all the details from May later.

Betty nodded. 'You won't believe what he was up to. Such a horrible man.'

Minty had no difficulty guessing what Mordecai had been doing. She'd known him as a young man. The only surprise was that he'd been alone in there.

'Darcy says Muriel thinks Humphrey went to the church to be closer to God when he died,' Betty said, rolling her eyes. 'As if Humphrey Oslac gave a tinker's toss about God.'

'Why do you think he died in the church?' Minty asked, sipping yet another cup of tea.

Betty shrugged. 'Who knows? I didn't know him well. I don't think anyone did, really. He just drove the 202 bus, bought fish and chips from the chippy on a Friday night and was usually in the The Crown on a Saturday. There's only his wife and mum to grieve him. You didn't hear it from me but, I don't think Muriel's heart is breaking. She's got her garden and the shop. But,' Betty leaned closer and lowered her voice, 'if you believe the gossip, there are women up and down the 202 route who'll be crying their eyes out tonight.'

'Is that so?' Minty said, feeling disgruntled to learn that she'd been one in a long line of dalliances.

'Couldn't keep it in his trousers.' Betty shook her head in disgust. 'Men! Why do we bother? Dedicate our lives to them and for what? Inevitable disappointment, that's what.'

Minty perked up her ears. Perhaps all wasn't as perfect as it seemed in Betty's immaculate life. Minty knew that before one could receive, it was usually necessary to give, so she said, 'I suppose May's father did his best, but Bertie was never a happy man. His mood affected everyone else's, so I'm afraid we didn't have a very joyful home. What about you and Chester? You were together a long time.'

'Mum never liked Chester. Never thought he was good enough,' Betty said, eyes hard. 'I always defended him but, in the end, Mum knew best.'

'I'm sorry to hear that,' Minty said. She remembered Betty's mother as a prissy, stuck-up little thing. It wasn't surprising that no one would be good enough for her daughter.

Betty sighed. 'God, I miss her so much.' Her eyes went soft and started to fill with tears. 'She was everything to me. I've been so lost without her.' Minty felt a twinge in her heart, knowing May would not feel the same once she'd gone.

'It takes time,' Minty said. 'You've suffered two huge losses in the last few months. Be kind to yourself. From what I see, you're doing wonderfully well.'

Betty sniffed, then blew her nose into a tissue that she tucked back up her sleeve. 'I think Jilly has the right answer.

Never get married. She does what she wants, when she wants, with no one to judge her or boss her around.'

Poor Betty. She'd obviously had a very unhappy marriage. Minty sympathised. 'What was your father like?' she asked.

Minty thought that people typically married someone similar to their most dominant parent. If Betty's husband was bossy and judgemental, who was he like? Her mother or her father? Minty's money was on the mother.

'Dad was a sweetheart,' Betty said, smiling. 'His head always stuck in a book. He taught at the comprehensive. Mum always said he should've tried for headmaster, that he wasn't living up to his full potential, but he was very happy with the students.' A cloud passed across her face. 'He just wanted a quiet life. I think that's why his death was easier to take. Whenever I think of him in the ground, I think "at least he's getting the peace he always wanted". Does that sound very silly?'

'No,' Minty said, nodding with understanding. 'That makes perfect sense.'

After Betty left, Minty took the tea things to the kitchen to wash up. May was sitting at the table staring into space. Mugs, crumbs, and newspapers were scattered across the tabletop.

'Sounds as if you and Fletcher sorted it all out with Humphrey,' Minty said. 'Betty was just telling me all about his body being found in the church this morning. What happened with Mordecai? Collateral damage?'

'Yes,' May replied without turning her head.

Minty set down the teacup she was rinsing and looked at May. 'I've decided to take up pole dancing,' she said. 'I hear it's a great way to get fit.'

May said nothing.

'And,' Minty continued, 'Betty thinks I could make a bit of pin money with an act at Stringfellows. What do you think?'

'Good idea,' May mumbled.

'Pollux May Morrigan!' Minty said. 'You haven't heard a word I've said.'

May jumped in her seat. 'Don't call me that. It makes me feel like a naughty three-year-old.' She turned to look at Minty. 'I still can't believe you let Bertie give us such ridiculous names. It always made us sound like fanatics or... or... *Americans*.'

'What's got your knickers in a twist?' Minty asked. 'You seem all out of sorts.' She pulled out a chair and sat across from May.

May glared at her with bloodshot eyes. 'Well, I've barely slept in the last two days. I need a shower and a long sleep.' She rubbed her face and yawned. 'Fletcher's been stabbed, I was up all night disposing of your dead lover, I saw a man wank himself to death, my mother keeps asking me to kill her, and there's a crazy person sending poisonous text messages and trying to kill people in the village. Have I forgotten anything?'

Minty wafted a hand around. 'I know about all that,' she said. 'Except the wanking. I assume that was Mordecai?'

May nodded.

'If you'd pull your finger out and help me, you could tick at least one of those things off your list,' Minty said. She pursed her lips and narrowed her eyes at May. 'There's something else though. Something you're not telling me.'

May stood up. 'Sparks is upstairs with Fletcher. I'm going to have a long, hot shower and then a nap,' she said. 'If you or Fletcher need me, you know where to find me, but please *don't* need me for the next four to six hours.' She left the kitchen mid-yawn.

Something was definitely up with May. Minty listened until

she heard May's bedroom door shut. Time to have a rummage around the library. If May was hiding something, signs of it would surely be there.

Minty shut the final drawer in May's desk. Apart from a wedding portrait shoved to the back of a drawer, she'd found nothing of interest, certainly no clue to whatever was bothering May. Leaning back in the desk chair, Minty turned in a slow circle, taking in the library.

It really was a beautiful room with thick rugs on the hardwood floor and a book-lined gallery overhead. The iron spiral staircase in the corner was particularly charming, though Minty thought she'd probably break an ankle if she tried to climb it. Then Minty remembered that the gallery had been created by knocking up into what had been *her* bedroom.

Her reflexive resentment quickly fizzled out. Who cares about a stupid bedroom? This was a much better use of the space.

She continued the circuit, admiring the fireplace, its mantle decorated with stuffed crows, the comfy furniture and the handsomely bound books in tidy rows. Parts of Greenway felt dated, mired in its own unhappy past, but this room was very much alive. It had a warmth and strength of character that was absent in so many rooms of the house. It was May's little nest, the space that she'd made most her own.

Minty continued turning until she ended up back where she'd started, facing May's desk and the glass cabinet beside it which held May's curiosities, bits and pieces picked up on her travels. She recognised a cannibal fork from Fiji, carved from dark wood and inlaid with mother-of-pearl. A wooden Native American doll decorated with feathers. The word *kachina* rose from the depths of Minty's mind. A tin mug with the name 'Gein' scrawled on it in marker pen. There, on the middle shelf, next to another morose little effigy, was a glass eye. Minty sat forward for a better look.

It wasn't just any glass eye. She could almost swear it was James Faraday's eye, the man who'd broken May's heart.

Minty opened a drawer and fished out the wedding portrait. May looked so beautiful with her long, dark hair around her shoulders. She'd worn a white suit like Bianca Jagger's, but May had taken it a step further and worn trousers on her wedding day. Scandalous. Now that Minty thought about it, it was perhaps the last time she'd seen May wear trousers. That is, until after James left. Trousers on women was probably another one of his controlling little pet peeves. God, she was growing to hate the man.

Holding the photo up to the light, she concentrated on James's eyes. There, the left pupil hadn't contracted in the bright sunlight, that must be the false eye. She looked closer. It was hazel, like the one in the cabinet. She compared the two. It could definitely be James's eye.

Minty looked out the window over the desk, but she wasn't seeing the heath or the church or the village. She was thinking of her daughter as a little girl, and of a little boy who'd made May angry by teasing her in front of the other children. A little boy who'd gone missing soon after, never to be seen again.

'Oh, my darling,' Minty said, looking at the photo of a once happy May. 'What have you done now?'

CHAPTER TWENTY-FOUR

GOOD VIBRATIONS

After his bath, Sparks had tucked Fletcher back into bed and told him to rest.

'Get some sleep,' he said. 'I'm teaching this afternoon, but I'll be back this evening to check on you.'

Fletcher tried to sleep, he really did, but he couldn't stop thinking about the latest text message. It could only be about May. He thought back over the numerous conversations they'd had in the last year. He'd once asked May directly if she'd killed James. Had she answered him?

He could picture that conversation. They'd been in the kitchen. She'd talked about James's secret family. They really existed. She'd found them on social media. But had she said that she'd definitely *not* killed James?

Fletcher couldn't be certain.

'Sod it,' he said. 'I'll just ask her.'

He grabbed his dressing gown and headed out on to the landing. May's bedroom door was shut, so she was probably inside. He raised his hand to knock, then froze when he noticed a strange electric buzzing sound coming from within. He leaned closer, curious about the odd noise, then heard May mumbling, 'Oh! Oh!'

Fletcher stepped back, eyes wide. 'Good for you, old girl,' he whispered, smiling to himself. His question could wait for a more convenient time.

Knowing he wouldn't be able to sleep until he spoke to May, he decided to go downstairs for a warm, milky drink. Perhaps that would help him nap through the afternoon. His arm ached under the sling and his eyes felt gritty. He *wanted* to sleep, he *needed* to sleep. It was just that his brain wasn't cooperating.

In the kitchen, he filled the milk pan and placed it on the Aga then took down the tin of Horlicks.

'I think I'll have one too,' Minty said, coming in and sitting at the table.

He prepared the drinks in their largest mugs, placed biscuits on a plate, then moved the newspapers aside and sat across from Minty. They clinked the mugs together.

'I heard about Mordecai,' Minty said, making the hand motion of a man masturbating.

'Yes,' Fletcher replied. 'It was very unpleasant and please don't ever make that gesture again. What have you been up to?' he asked, setting his drink on the table to cool and helping himself to a chocolate bourbon.

'Betty popped round for a chat. She was full of news from the village. All about Humphrey and Mordecai.' She made eye contact with Fletcher before repeating the hand gesture, then took a custard cream from the plate.

Fletcher chose to ignore it. Humphrey and the tunnels seemed like yonks ago. Hard to believe it had only been a few hours since they were hiding in that utility room.

'Did you get a look at his you-know-what?' Minty asked, waggling her eyebrows.

Fletcher nodded, desperate to change the subject. He was in no mood to talk todgers with Minty.

'What did I tell you?' she said. 'The old Hobby Horse had a way with the ladies.'

'How was Betty?' Fletcher asked.

'She sends her best wishes to you about the newspaper article,' Minty said, obviously reluctant to change the subject, but taking the hint. 'How are you feeling about that?'

'I have no idea,' he replied, relieved at the change of topic. He reached for a Jammie Dodger this time. 'I knew this day would come. I used to imagine it, but I always thought I'd *feel* more when it happened. I just feel numb.' He tried to sip his Horlicks, but it was still too hot. He dunked his biscuit before taking a bite.

Minty folded her hands together on the scarred pine tabletop. The table had been part of Greenway since before Minty was born. Did she feel that connection when she placed her hands on it, or perhaps it just became invisible with familiarity?

'I'm going to be honest with you,' she said. 'Just tell me to shut up if I sound like an old fool.' She cleared her throat and gathered her thoughts. 'I've always thought that Barb was the mother you needed, that you and May both needed. She came at a time when you'd left home and were finding your feet. Barbara filled the space where your mother and I, for different reasons, were inadequate.'

'Oh, Minty.' Fletcher reached across the table. He felt something inside of himself giving way. 'That's not true.'

She swatted his hands away, which reminded him of May. 'Don't "Oh, Minty" me,' she said. 'I'm too old to lie to myself. I was a terrible mother. There may have been good reasons for that, but the end result was the same. I was *not* a good mother. But Barbara Bouvier was. She was ballsy and sentimental. She was warm, affectionate and funny. She was all the things you needed and wanted from a mother and I'm so glad she came into your lives. But...' She stopped and seemed to reflect before continuing.

Fletcher leaned forward, not wanting to miss a single word.

'Perhaps,' Minty said, 'you don't need a mother anymore.'

Fletcher sat back in his chair. Instead of bursting forth with a bang, the feeling that had been growing in his chest simply let go with a gentle sigh.

'For an old fool, you're very insightful,' he said. He reached again to take Minty's hand. This time she let him. He'd been fascinated by Minty's hands when he was younger. They'd been so pale, with long, red nails. Now they were wrinkled, covered in age spots, the fingers slightly twisted with arthritis. The once red nails were ridged and yellow, though still perfectly maintained.

'Minty,' he said. 'Do you remember once when I came to visit, you put your hand on my knee and said I should let you know if there was anything I needed?'

To his surprise, Minty blushed. 'Yes,' she replied. 'I'm sorry for that. I was deep into the G&Ts at the time, but that's no excuse.'

'Did you know that Bertie did the same?' Fletcher asked.

Minty looked him in the face, raising both of her pencilled brows. 'No, I didn't.' She looked away before asking, 'Does May know?'

Fletcher shook his head. 'No. I was an adult. It was just the once and nothing ever came of it. No harm done. Their relationship was difficult enough without adding more trouble to the mix.' He looked at Minty. 'Was Bertie gay? Was that why he was such an angry man? I know it would've been impossible for him to live openly back then.'

Minty sighed. 'Yes, Bertie was a complicated man. I'm sure

his sexuality felt like an additional burden. I knew the situation when we married and it did mean that he never came near *me*, for which I was grateful.' Her eyes became sad as she revisited her past and, for a moment, Fletcher could see the beautiful, despondent woman who seemed to haunt Greenway during his early visits there.

'Not never,' he said softly, careful not to disturb her reverie, but feeling this was an opportunity he couldn't pass up. 'You did have a family.'

Minty snapped back to the present. 'Yes, of course. Thankfully, once was all it took.' She picked up her mug and took a big sip.

Fletcher and May had realised long ago that Minty must've already been pregnant when she married Bertie. The dates didn't add up. They'd assumed that this need to marry was what had forced the unsuitable couple together, not unusual for the time. The idea of Minty falling pregnant before marriage hadn't come as a shock, but now Fletcher wondered if there was more to it. Was Bertie May's father at all?

'Any more of those strange phone messages come through?' Minty asked in an obvious attempt to change the subject.

Perhaps Minty would be a good person with whom to discuss the possible fate of James? Who else could Fletcher possibly talk to about it? But did Minty really know about May's murderous past, or was all her talk of death just tongue-in-cheek?

'There was another text this morning,' he said, fishing around in his dressing gown pocket for his phone. He found the text from Bastian and handed the phone to Minty.

Minty's face froze when she read the text. 'To whom is this one referring?' she asked, her eyes not leaving the screen.

'I'm not sure,' Fletcher replied. He sipped his Horlicks, which was finally the perfect temperature, and watched her.

Minty's nose twitched like a cornered mouse. She suspected May too. He could tell. 'Who do *you* think it might be about?' he asked.

'How should I know?' she said, handing the phone back and making an exaggerated face of confusion.

As Fletcher took the phone, they made eye contact.

'You think it's about May,' they said at the same time.

'Don't be ridiculous,' they said.

Fletcher held up his good hand. Minty snapped her mouth shut. 'Don't say anything else,' he said. 'Why do you think the text could refer to May?'

'I don't think that,' Minty said.

'Come now, you just told me you're too old to lie to yourself. You obviously think May killed James. Why? Do you have proof?'

Minty looked away, then back at Fletcher. She grimaced, then huffed. 'You know the display case in the library?'

Fletcher nodded.

'When did you last look at it?' Minty asked. 'I mean, really look. Can you think of anything odd in it?'

'It's all odd,' Fletcher said, blanching. 'I don't *want* to know what half the things are in there. May has some unusual interests. But you're talking about something specific. What is it?' He realised that he'd started whispering in case May heard them.

'An eye,' Minty said, whispering as well. 'A *glass* eye.'

Fletcher's mouth fell open. He knew only one person with a glass eye and that person was *never* seen without it.

James.

May banged into the kitchen, her face pink and scowling. 'What are you two gossiping about in here?' she said.

CHAPTER TWENTY-FIVE

GOD ONLY KNOWS

When May floated back into consciousness, soft light was creeping round the edges of her bedroom curtains. She looked at the clock and realised she'd slept almost twelve hours. The previous afternoon, after showering and trying out her new face-shaving gadget (which hurt like a motherfucker), she'd gone down to the kitchen for something sweet. Minty and Fletcher had been huddled together over the kitchen table. They'd shared an oddly quiet snack in the kitchen, then she'd filled the dog bowls and gone back to bed.

The dogs.

May sat up, knowing she'd find yellow puddles and piles of poop in the kitchen if no one had thought to let them out. Sweet George seemed to choose an out-of-the-way place, like in the corner, for her 'accidents', but Bess would plant her flag right inside the kitchen door where it would definitely be trod in or smeared across the floor when the door was opened. Not the best way to start the day.

May touched her upper lip. It still felt sore, as if she'd been sunburned. The horrid shaver, which pulled the hair out at the roots, had been tossed in the bathroom bin. Life was too short for that kind of pain.

Throwing on her robe, she decided to face the worst before getting dressed, and headed to the kitchen. She opened the door slowly, peeking around to check for puddles. All clear.

Phew. Someone must've let the dogs out. Their bowls were full of kibble, though Bess and George were nowhere to be seen. They would be with Minty or Fletcher.

May relaxed a little and made a pot of coffee. She still appreciated the way that Fletcher would step in when she was occupied or under the weather. The first year after James left, May had been 'under the weather' quite a lot. Whole weeks had passed in a kind of dark fog. Fletcher had always been there with food and drinks, caring for the dogs, running the house in May's absence. It was such a contrast to James, who required detailed lists any time May was away or ill. Even then, when she returned or recovered there would be piles of washing to be done, tasks that had been ignored. It felt like a punishment for needing any time for herself. There was always a price to pay.

James couldn't locate things in their own home, though they'd lived there for decades. When he unloaded the dishwasher, May would find items left on the side because he'd say he didn't know where they went, though they were always stored in the same place. Since he'd left, May had come to realise that James had been a passenger in their life together, never fully engaging. He skimmed the surface of life, dipping in for the good things, focussing on his own interests, never taking responsibility for the mundane details or carrying the emotional load. Those were left to May.

After forty years, he'd left with a suitcase and a cardboard box, taking no souvenirs from their travels, no photos. He seemed to have no attachment at all to the four decades they'd spent together. She imagined him unplugging himself from his life at Greenway, then slotting into life with the other woman. Shedding the identity he'd worn with May to put on a different ill-fitting version of himself.

May had walked through the house after his departure and realised what little impact his absence actually made, apart from the gaping hole in her own heart. She'd lived alone within their marriage for years.

Then Fletcher had come and allowed May to fall apart. She'd spent days in bed, drifting in and out of sleep while Fletcher and Jilly cooked, cleaned, and reorganised the house. Fletcher now knew Greenway almost as well as May did.

She picked up her phone and opened Spring Chicken. After ripping all the hair off her face the day before, she'd gritted her teeth and downloaded a dating app for people over fifty. The name of it made her cringe, but it was apparently very popular. May scanned the profiles, swiping left on each one. None of the men looked remotely interesting. Most of the photos seemed to be years old, usually taken in some holiday destination. One man had posted a black-and-white photo that must've been taken before the turn of the millennium. It seemed hopeless, but May was determined.

She'd written her own profile the day before but hadn't yet posted it. When she read through it now, it sounded boring and pretentious. The guidelines had said to 'Be bold! Be unique! Use emojis! Don't be afraid to stand out!'. It made May vomit a little bit in the back of her throat.

She clicked the cursor... delete... delete... delete... removing the details of her career as a librarian, her world travels, her love of gardening, her bookshop. Surely, she could come up with something better.

'What time did you tell the others to be here?' Fletcher said, coming into the kitchen. He was still in his dressing gown.

May fumbled with her phone, dropping it in her lap. 'Eight,' she said. She'd texted for Bastian and Sparks to come round for breakfast so they could talk about the newest developments, because she and Fletcher had been too tired to meet up the previous evening.

'How did you sleep?' Fletcher asked, sitting at the table after pouring a cup of coffee from the pot.

'Marvellously,' she replied.

'Me too,' Fletcher said. 'I feel like a new man.' He circled his shoulder carefully. 'Hopefully we'll make some progress on our malicious messenger today.'

'Thanks for feeding the dogs,' May said, nodding towards the full bowls.

Fletcher shook his head. 'Wasn't me. Must've been Minty. I've been down for the count since we left the kitchen yesterday afternoon.'

'Minty must be adjusting to communal living at last,' May replied.

An hour later, May was in her library feeling fresh and clear-headed for the first time in days. She'd showered, and dressed in navy trousers and a pretty Barbara Hulanicki tunic found in the back of her wardrobe. Going to her Kelly bag on the shelf outside the library, she extracted her phone, then broke her own rule by taking it into the library. Posing in front of the nearest bookshelf, she took a quick selfie and loaded it to her Spring Chicken profile. The clink of china could be heard coming from the kitchen, so she quickly chose a few emojis then, before she could second-guess herself, hit 'Share', posting her profile to the app. She just managed to chuck the phone back into her bag before the doorbell rang.

Barb came round the corner wearing an Yves Saint Laurent

kaftan, pushing the drinks trolley with her good hand. She was using an Hermès scarf as a jaunty sling.

'Have you seen Minty?' Barb said, as May went to answer the door.

'No.' May stopped, one hand on the door handle. 'You haven't seen her at all?'

Barb shook her head. 'Not since yesterday. I'll check her room.'

CHAPTER TWENTY-SIX

WHO'S THAT LADY?

'Minty sends her apologies,' Barb said, joining May, Sparks and Bastian in the library. 'Said she was awake most of the night and didn't fall asleep until the sun was coming up.' She perched on an armchair. 'She may join us later, if we're lucky.'

'Fine,' May replied. 'Does everyone have something to drink?'

The group helped themselves to pastries and the still-warm quiche Lorraine, made by Sparks that morning. Bastian looked pensive as May distributed forks and napkins along with the details of the most recent message.

'I came by last night,' Sparks said to Barb, 'but you were asleep, and I thought it best not to wake you.'

Barb smiled. 'I'm glad you didn't.' She kissed him on the nose. 'I feel much better after that long sleep.'

They looked at the page May had given them.

Fifth message:

Suspicion haunts the guilty mind. I know you killed your husband. Where is he now?

Henry VI, said by Gloucester to King Henry in Act 5, Scene 6

'Suspicion always haunts the guilty mind; the thief doth fear each bush and officer.'

No initials again.

'No confusion about the meaning of this one,' Sparks said. 'But to whom is it directed? No initials to give us a clue this time.'

Barb kept her eyes glued to the page.

'There are a number of widows in Blackheath,' May replied. 'If the sender is just fishing around, I suppose it could apply to any of them. Maybe that's what the lack of initials means. That those messages aren't directed to any one person? Were there incidents or accidents last night after the text was sent?' She turned to Bastian.

Bastian shook his head. 'Not that I've heard about.'

Barb looked up and said, 'What about husbands who've gone missing? Do we have any of those in the village?' She glanced at the display case beside the desk where the glass eye seemed to be glaring at her, then locked eyes with May.

'None that I can think of,' May said, unblinking.

Barb wished that Minty was there. She'd probably blurt out their suspicions. Or maybe it was best to wait until they were alone. She lowered her eyes again.

'Yesterday there were people waiting on the pavement outside the shop,' May said. 'Did they receive the text as well?'

Bastian nodded. 'I know some of them did.'

'Does that mean the sender could also be outside the shop when the message is sent?' May asked.

Bastian nodded again. 'I've been thinking along the same lines. It's all about the reach of their Bluetooth. They could be in the shop, out front, in the alley behind.' He shrugged. 'It's impossible to know for sure.'

Sparks, always keen on anything to do with technology or gadgets, sat forward. 'What about creating a Faraday cage around the shop?' he asked. 'At least that would exclude the bookshop from the circus that's growing around the texts.'

'I'm not sure we want to do that,' Bastian replied. 'We now have some idea of the vicinity of the sender. If they move somewhere else, it doesn't stop them, but it does make our job more difficult.'

Barb squirmed on the sofa beside Sparks. For some reason, it all felt remarkably boring.

'Are the police taking the texts seriously?' May asked.

Bastian sighed. 'Nope. They still think they're some kind of prank and that there's no link to Juan's death or Fletcher's attack. Do we think the deaths of Humphrey Oslac and Mordecai Page are a part of this?'

'No,' May and Barb said at the same time.

Bastian looked from one to the other. 'The message could refer to Humphrey's wife. Could Muriel have killed him?'

'No,' they said again.

'The timing doesn't work,' May quickly clarified. 'Humphrey was dead and discovered before the message about dead husbands was sent. And the text before that clearly referred to Clementine Kirkland, so it wasn't related to Humphrey or Mordecai either. I heard from Jean, by the way, and they're all fine. I think getting them away was the right thing to do.'

'Two bodies in the church seems like a strange coincidence,'

Bastian said. 'I don't think we should ignore the possibility that they're related.'

Barb's heart was pounding in her chest. She looked to May.

'Yes,' May said. 'You're absolutely right. We shouldn't ignore them, but at the moment I don't see how they would fit in with the messages. Do you?'

Bastian thought a moment before shaking his head.

'So, we won't ignore them,' May continued. 'At the moment, we simply can't see any connection to the texts or the other attacks.'

Barb's heart rate returned to normal.

The discussion went round in circles with Barb fidgeting, rearranging her dress and adjusting her earrings every few seconds. When Bastian left to open the bookshop and May took the trolley back to the kitchen, Sparks turned to Barb.

'Are you okay?' he said. 'You seem restless.'

Barb tossed her hair, prepared to say something saucy in reply, then slumped against the sofa. 'It's not the same,' she said, using Fletcher's deeper voice. 'That damn woman!'

'Which woman?' Sparks asked, taking Fletcher's hand.

'The journalist,' he said. 'Before that story, when I was Barb, I *was* Barb. Now it feels like I'm Fletcher *pretending* to be Barb. It feels wrong. Does that make sense?'

Sparks nodded. 'You know I don't care what you call yourself or how you dress. It's the same spirit underneath it all. That's who I want to spend time with.'

He nodded and reached up to stroke Sparks's sweet face, causing Barb's bracelets to jingle. Fletcher glared at them, took them off and slammed them down on the side table. 'Goddamnit,' he said. 'I don't know what to do.'

'I think you're in a strong position,' Sparks said. 'This journalist is way out of line. You can tell your side of the story, possibly even sue her for invasion of privacy. You would be held up as an example in the LGBTQ+ community.'

Fletcher grimaced. 'I've thought about all that,' he said. 'To be honest, being a role model sounds like a lot of hard work. Maybe if I was twenty years younger, but not now.' He looked at Sparks. 'Right now, all I really want to do is read my books, spend time with you, get into trouble with May and eat some delicious cakes every now and then.'

'Come away with me this weekend,' Sparks said. 'You can meet the whole extended Chanda family.' He laughed. 'I'm not saying it won't be stressful, but it'll be a different kind of stress. The change would do you good. Besides, I want you to meet my family. They'll love you.'

Fletcher laid his head on Sparks's broad shoulder. 'I'd like that, but not this weekend. May needs me here and I need to decide what I'm going to do about this journalist.'

Sparks leaned forward to kiss the top of Fletcher's head just as a chicken clucked nearby.

Buk, buk, ba-GAWK.

CHAPTER TWENTY-SEVEN

DO THE FUNKY CHICKEN

Fletcher and Sparks sat up and looked around the room in confusion as the sound came again.

Buk, buk, ba-GAWK.

'What on earth?' Fletcher said, standing up to locate the source of the sound.

Buk, buk, ba-GAWK.

Buk, buk, ba-GAWK.

The two men traced the noise to May's handbag sitting on the shelf outside the library door. They were staring at it when May returned.

Buk, buk, ba-GAWK.

Buk, buk, ba-GAWK.

'Oh, for fuck's sake!' May said, snatching her mobile from the bag and switching it to silent.

Sparks started smiling. 'Spring Chicken? It sounds like you've got quite a few admirers.'

May had gone pink with embarrassment.

'Spring Chicken?' Fletcher said. 'What's that?'

May held the phone against her chest as it continued to

vibrate with notifications. 'I was just going to ask if either of you wanted another drink,' she said.

'Oh, no,' Fletcher said. 'Not until you tell me what Spring Chicken is.'

'Fine,' May replied, her mouth a hard line. 'Let's go to the kitchen for this. I need a proper drink.'

Sparks was grinning like an idiot, as Fletcher followed them to the kitchen, dismayed and intrigued by their reactions.

'You explain it to Fletcher while I make the drinks,' May said. 'Bloody Marys?' She prepared glasses with vodka, tomato juice, Worcestershire sauce, Tabasco and celery salt. May was cutting celery into sticks when Minty joined them.

'My favourite breakfast,' Minty said, nodding at the drinks lined up on the counter. 'You really shouldn't have.' She shuffled into the kitchen, still sleepy, looking more than ever like ET without her wig and make-up. May set out another glass.

'It's a dating app for people over fifty,' Sparks was saying. 'It's called Spring Chicken and whenever someone messages you or shows an interest, the app makes that clucking sound.'

Minty raised her eyebrows, or rather she raised the part of her forehead where her eyebrows would be once she'd drawn them on. 'For over fifties, you say?'

'Don't get any ideas,' May replied, giving Minty a stern look.

'So, Ms Morrigan,' Sparks said. 'Let's see your profile. It's obviously a good one to get that kind of response.'

May distributed the cocktails before responding. 'Absolutely not,' she said, taking a long sip.

Fletcher had removed Barb's wig from his head and set it on the table beside his drink. 'Go on, I could do with a laugh.'

'*Definitely* not after that remark,' May said, gripping her phone closer.

Sparks stirred his drink with a celery stick. 'I could be very naughty and reactivate my profile, then find yours.' He gave a wicked laugh.

'Do it, do it,' Fletcher said, egging him on.

May rolled her eyes. 'You're like a couple of schoolboys.' Shaking her head, she opened her profile in the app and handed the phone across the table. 'If you must,' she said. The phone continued to vibrate with responses.

Minty stood behind Sparks so she could read over his shoulder. 'Lovely photo,' she said. 'You can't see your moustache at all. What's all those things at the bottom though? It's all jibber jabber.'

'They're emojis,' May said. 'You're supposed to put them on your profile to make it more interesting. Everyone seems to do it.'

Fletcher realised that Sparks had gone bright red and was struggling to keep himself together. The phone was shaking in his hands.

'May,' Sparks squeaked, 'what do you think these emojis mean?' He swallowed hard and held out the phone.

May gave him a funny look. 'The waving hand means hello. The aubergine and the tulip are because I enjoy gardening.' She pointed to each symbol as if explaining to a small child.

Sparks snorted. Tears had started to roll down his cheeks. 'Go on,' he said, almost gasping for air.

'The camel is for my travels, the books are for the bookshop and my career as a librarian,' she continued.

'And the unicorn?' Sparks could barely get the words out.

'I don't know.' May shrugged. 'I thought it was whimsical. The guidelines said to make yourself stand out.'

'Well, you've certainly done that,' Sparks said, clearing his throat and wiping his eyes. He pointed to May's phone. 'These emojis have very specific meanings in online dating.' He pointed at the aubergine and tulip. 'These represent male and female genitals.'

Minty leaned in for a closer look.

'That's ridiculous,' May said, turning pink.

'The waving hand usually refers to... well, spanking,' Sparks continued. Fletcher snorted beside him. 'And the camel,' he continued. 'Camels have humps, so you can imagine what that means.'

May groaned and placed her forehead on the table in utter defeat. 'What about the books?' she asked. 'What the bloody hell do the books mean?'

'The books are fine,' Sparks replied. 'The books have no other meaning that I know of.'

May raised her head. 'Thank God for that.'

'But.' Sparks held up a finger, halting any sense of consolation May might've been feeling. 'The unicorn.' He looked up at May. 'The unicorn...' He spluttered as he tried to get the words out. 'The unicorn means... means...'

'Come on,' Fletcher said. 'The suspense is killing me.'

Sparks composed himself. 'The unicorn stands for... a bisexual woman looking for a threesome.'

Fletcher chuckled. 'Maybe forty years ago...'

'You're making this up,' May said. 'How can a unicorn possibly represent a threesome?'

Sparks held up both hands. 'I don't make the rules,' he said.

Minty took the phone from his hand. 'So, by your interpretation this message says "spank, cock, fanny, hump, books, up for a threesome"? No wonder you're so popular.'

'And,' Sparks added with a flourish, 'is that the *Kama Sutra* on the bookshelf behind you in the photo?'

May snatched the phone from Minty's hand. She tapped at the screen. 'Thank you all very much. I'm deleting this app right now. What a bloody nightmare.'

'Don't do that,' Fletcher said, wiping tears from his eyes. 'Just change your profile. I'm sure you can block any weirdos who got in touch.'

May emptied her glass. 'I need some fresh air,' she said. 'I'll take the dogs for a walk.' She left the kitchen to find Bess and George.

As soon as May was gone, the remaining three fell about laughing.

'Oh, my days,' Fletcher said, wiping his eyes. 'I needed that.'

May returned, carrying the dog leads and looking frustrated. 'Has anyone seen the dogs?' she asked. Everyone at the table shook their heads.

'Didn't you feed them this morning?' May asked Minty.

'Not me,' Minty said. 'I haven't seen them since yesterday.'

May looked at the bowls full of kibble beside the Aga. 'Then, that must be the same food I put down yesterday.'

The four of them searched Greenway top to bottom. May checked the cellar. Minty walked through the ground floor calling their names. Fletcher looked upstairs and hunted for holes in the garden fence. Sparks inspected the front garden and surveyed the heath, but it was no use.

Bess and George were gone.

CHAPTER TWENTY-EIGHT

BEGIN THE BEGUINE

Minty wanted to go back to bed. May had been going on about the blasted dogs for what felt like days. She looked at the mantel clock. It had actually been less than fifteen minutes.

The lovely Sparks had left, full of apologies, for his family's Easter reunion on the coast, leaving Minty with a worried Fletcher and an increasingly annoying May.

'Where the hell can they be?' May said for the thousandth time, pacing back and forth in the library. She turned to Minty. 'Go over it again. Who came to the house while Fletcher and I were sleeping? Don't leave anyone out.'

Minty sighed. 'I've already said, just Betty was here yesterday. She came for our usual chat. That's it.'

'The post was on the hall table,' May said. 'Did you open the door for the postman?'

'Ah, yes. That's right.' Minty remembered now. 'The postman did knock, and I opened the door to him. Did you know he's a musician? Plays in a band at–'

'So, you stood at the door nattering to the postman?' May

interrupted. 'That must be what happened. The dogs ran out when the door was open.'

'No.' Minty shook her head. 'That can't be right. I took them out on the heath *after* the postman had come.'

'I think,' Fletcher said, 'if they'd run out at any point, they would've come home by now.'

'Yes,' May agreed with a sigh. 'George, in particular, would be wanting her bed after a little adventure. They'd surely be recognised on the heath or in the village. If they just wandered off, someone would've brought them back.'

Fletcher sat up suddenly. 'Oh my God, someone's snatched them up and will be selling them online. Do you know how much dachshunds go for these days? They're being trafficked!'

Minty's head ached from all the drama.

'I'll speak to Bastian,' May said. 'He must have some way of monitoring online ads. If anyone tries to sell Bess or George, he'll find them.'

'Virgilia said she saw a dachshund for sale for £10,000,' Minty said. Mind-boggling what someone would pay for a dog. 'Imagine that, a £10,000 dog. You'd think he'd have gold bollocks or something.'

'Should we contact the police?' Fletcher asked. 'Does the canine unit cover dognappings?'

'A silver dapple like George could go for even more if she can be used for breeding,' Minty continued.

'I don't think so,' May replied to Fletcher. 'But we should report it.'

'Virgilia said there's something called a double dapple that people go mad for,' Minty said. 'The sky's the limit when it comes to double dapples, even though it's a wicked thing to do to a dog.'

May turned to Minty. 'What on earth are you babbling about?' she asked.

'They have lots of birth defects,' Minty said. 'The Kennel Club refuses to register them.'

'Who?' May said.

'Double-dapple dachshunds,' Minty replied.

'Fuck's sake,' Fletcher said. 'Are you seriously having a stroke, Minty?'

Minty sighed and rolled her eyes. 'Virgilia told me all about it. You can't breed two dapples or–'

'Who's Virgilia?' May asked, perturbed at this random detour into Minty-land.

Minty sat up straighter, lifting her chin. May could be so rude. 'Your cleaning lady,' she said. 'Do you never speak to your staff?'

'I don't have staff,' May replied. 'When did you talk to her?'

'If you must know,' Minty said, 'she stopped by yesterday to say she's going away, so she won't be able to clean for you next week.'

'Yesterday?' May said. 'So, Jilly stopped by as well? And you'd forgotten that until now? Good grief, did half the village come to the house yesterday?'

Minty squinted and pressed her lips together. 'Did I mention that the vicar came by to check on Fletcher?'

'For God's sake!' May shouted. 'How many other visitors have you forgotten?'

'And that lovely Sparks popped in later, but Fletcher was asleep.' Minty cringed inside herself. She really had forgotten.

Fletcher was sitting in an armchair by the fireplace, staring into space. 'Virgilia?' he said. 'Jilly's name is Virgilia? You know that for a fact?'

'Yes.' Minty nodded. 'She said her father chose the name. Jilly laughed about it, saying how wrong he'd been about her.' She shrugged.

Fletcher turned to May. 'Virgilia,' he said. '*Coriolanus*. "My gracious silence".'

May turned white and sat down on the sofa. Minty saw the line between May's eyes deepen. She really should consider a touch of Botox. 'Jilly?' May said.

Minty looked from Fletcher to May. They both seemed stunned. She sipped her second Bloody Mary, now watery with melting ice and in need of a top-up.

'Did you say Jilly's gone away?' May asked.

Minty nodded, fishing out the celery stick with her fingers.

'Did she say where she's going?' Fletcher asked.

Minty crunched the celery and shook her head. 'No idea,' she replied.

'We need to get inside Jilly's house,' May said, standing up. 'I'll bring my lockpicks.'

'I'm coming with you,' Fletcher said. 'Give me a minute to change.' He was still wearing Barb's kaftan.

Minty found a nail file in the pocket of her dressing gown and began to file her nails. From the corner of her eye she could see May hovering in the library doorway. 'You don't know where Jilly lives, do you?' Minty tutted and shook her head.

'It won't be difficult to find out,' May replied.

Minty tutted again. 'You really should pay more attention to the people you employ.' She continued to file her nails. 'She still lives in her father's house. Inherited it when he died. Pretty place, I believe, though it needs a bit of work.'

'Right,' May said, still lingering in the doorway. 'Are you going to keep dropping clues or will you give me the bloody address?'

'It's 77 Bennett Park,' Minty said.

'Thank you,' May replied, grabbing her jacket from the hook in the hallway.

Minty stopped filing to look at May. 'Her neighbour was

burgled a few months ago, so Jilly had new locks installed. High tech. Unpickable.'

'We'll see about that,' May said.

But,' Minty continued, 'Betty has a fob. I think that's what she called it.'

'Why does Betty have a key to Jilly's house?' May asked.

Minty despaired sometimes, she really did. 'Betty Danvers is the most trustworthy person in the village,' she said. 'She has emergency keys to half the houses in Blackheath.'

Fletcher joined them, wearing a shirt and tweed blazer with his arm back in its proper sling.

May opened the front door and a roar went up outside.

'Dr Redmond!'

'Dr Redmond, this way! Look this way!'

'Dr Redmond, what do you have to say about this article claiming you're Barbara Bouvier?'

'Dr Redmond! Dr Redmond!'

May slammed the door shut with a bang.

Minty went to the library window for a better look. 'Looks like the cat's well and truly out of the bag now,' she said, raising her empty glass to toast the swarm of journalists gathered in front of Greenway.

CHAPTER TWENTY-NINE

BORN TO BE WILD

'We'll have to go out the back way,' May said. The crowd had quieted down once she'd shut the door. They obviously knew the rules and remained off Greenway's lawn, congregating on the public heath in front of the house. This was both a good thing and a bad thing. It meant they weren't knocking on the door or peeking in the windows, but it also meant that May couldn't ask the police to remove them.

Minty was pressed against the glass of the library window, watching the journalists. 'You'll still have to run the gauntlet, even from the back,' she said. 'There's a group of them moving down towards the alley now.'

'Bloody hell,' May said. 'I'm not hiding in here all day when Bess and George are out there somewhere.' She turned to Fletcher. 'You stay here. They're not interested in me. I'll push through and get to Jilly's.'

'I suppose I could make a statement,' Fletcher said, his face pale and hands shaking. 'Maybe they'd go away after that.'

This was clearly not something Fletcher wanted to do.

'No,' May replied. 'Don't let them bully you into doing

something you don't want to do. I'll be fine.' She adjusted her jacket, preparing for the onslaught.

'Wait!' Fletcher said. 'If Jilly is behind the texts, then she's capable of violence.' He nodded towards his shoulder. 'I can't let you go alone.'

May knew that she could defend herself just fine on her own, but she didn't want to leave Fletcher with the baying masses outside. He would do nothing but fret while she was gone, then most likely, throw himself on the mercy of the crowd.

'What about the tunnels?' Minty said.

May shook her head, thinking it over. 'Pilates, the nursery, and the cooking class in the crypt today.' Then a slow smile spread across her face. 'I know a way we can get out of here,' she said.

The motorbike shot through the throng of journalists gathered around the opening to the alleyway. The two riders, clad in riding leathers and helmets, were a blur.

'I told you this would work,' May said, talking via her helmet's Bluetooth speaker as she leaned into a tight left around the edge of the heath.

Once Fletcher stopped screaming, he agreed that the ploy had been effective. 'Jilly's place was just ahead, where are you going?' he shouted.

'No need to shout,' May replied. 'The helmet microphones are sensitive. I'm going to make a quick circuit, just to make sure no one is following us.' She turned towards Prince of Wales Road and accelerated. Fletcher yelped, gripping her waist with his good arm.

May had won the 1964 Triumph Bonneville in a bet when she and Fletcher were students at Cambridge. She'd immediately christened the bike 'Patsy'. It was one of the great loves of her life. Through May's attentive care and maintenance, Patsy still looked factory fresh.

The engine roared as she took the Sun in the Sands roundabout at speed.

'You're just taking the piss now!' Fletcher shrieked. 'I'm one-handed back here. May Morrigan, I can hear you laughing!'

May switched off her mic and headed back towards Blackheath Village, shoulders shaking with glee. Patsy always brought out the worst in her.

In Bennett Park, they came to a stop outside number 77. The four-storey semi had once been a fine home. Grand, even. Compared to its neighbours, it was now in a state of disrepair. The brickwork was dark with grime, the masonry chipped and peeling, the paved front garden cracked and overgrown with weeds. At some point in the distant past, the steps leading up to the front door had been covered in asphalt which had been left to sag and tear, revealing crumbling concrete underneath. Stained blinds were drawn on all of the upstairs windows. Only the barred basement windows displayed floral curtains, which were closed tight. A hanging planter full of fresh blooms hung beside the basement door.

'Jilly lives in this place on her own?' Fletcher asked as he carefully dismounted, leathers creaking with the movement.

May took off her helmet, rubbed at her hip and nodded. 'Since her father died. I knew she'd grown up in Blackheath. I hadn't realised that she lived in the heart of the village.'

Tucked away off the main village thoroughfare, Bennett Park was made up of large period homes, most of them divided into one- and two-bed flats. The street had once been the village's centre of creativity with the former Blackheath Arts Club (now a block of flats) at one end and the The Old Bakehouse Theatre at the other. The theatre was currently managed by the Blackheath Age Exchange and hosted various events including the popular second-hand book sale.

'Seems like an enormous house for one person,' Fletcher said. 'I wonder why she doesn't sell up. She'd make a packet on this place. Could live anywhere she wanted.'

'It's her home,' May replied. 'The only home she's ever known.' She took one look at the porch and steps, strewn with leaves and muck, then, unstrapping her handbag from Patsy's parcel shelf, May pushed open the gate and headed towards the basement door. The gate screeched on rusting hinges.

'She knows we're coming,' Fletcher said.

'That's fine with me,' May replied, patting her sleeve where she'd concealed a small blade. The stiletto knife was one of a pair, given to her by an admirer many years before, so sharp and fine it went in like butter. 'I'm always prepared.'

May knocked at the glossy red basement door. There was no answer. She knocked again, then lifted the letterbox flap and shouted through the opening. 'Jilly! It's May Morrigan. Are you there?' Still no reply. Looking through the letterbox revealed a tidy narrow hallway with a faded runner that ended in a closed door. She sniffed. No cooking smells, no doggy odours, nothing except a whiff of the pine-scented cleaner Jilly preferred.

'Looks like no one's home,' Fletcher said, still standing on the steps, as there wasn't space enough for two in the basement's tiny porch.

May rifled through her handbag until she found her lockpicks. 'We'll soon know for sure,' she said, turning back to the door. 'Bugger. She's got one of those keyless locks.'

'You can't pick those?' Fletcher asked, trying to peer over May's shoulder.

'There's nothing to pick,' she said. 'No keyhole. This one doesn't even have a number pad.' She examined the door, then the windows. 'The door hinges are on the interior, so I can't remove them to get inside. The windows are all painted shut. Even if we broke a pane, I couldn't squeeze between those bars. Could you?' She turned to Fletcher.

He was shaking his head. 'Not in a million years,' he replied, eyeing the rusty metal bars covering each window.

May took out her phone and photographed the door, its lock and handle. 'Maybe Bastian can help with this,' she said. She turned back to the windows. 'We'd need a saw to get through those bars. Hacksaw or an angle grinder, diamond blade,' May muttered, half to herself. 'Maybe a blowtorch.'

'Did you just say *blowtorch*?' Fletcher asked, wide-eyed.

May ignored the question. 'Let's go check the other door.' She pushed past Fletcher, heading for the grotty steps.

The main door to the house hadn't been used for some time. The porch was filthy, with skeletons of leaves from autumns past piled in the corners and cobwebs across every surface, apart from the area that had been wiped clean in order to install the new keyless door handle.

'Buggery hell!' May said. 'What has she got in there that's so important? It's like bloody Fort Knox.' May photographed that door and its lock before knocking loudly, causing a curl of faded black paint to detach and flutter to the ground. She lifted the rusty letterbox flap. 'Jilly!' she shouted through the opening. 'Bess! George! Walkies!' She put her ear to the flap and listened closely. Nothing. No scuffling, no whining, no barking. If the dogs were there, surely they would make a noise. Unless...

May shook the thought from her head. No. The dogs would be fine. What kind of monster could hurt such tiny, defenceless animals? Human beings were one thing, but dogs? No. May wouldn't allow herself to believe that the dogs had come to any harm.

Looking through the letterbox, she could make out an ornate hallway covered in dust and cobwebs. Scrutinising the dust,

May could see that it was disturbed near the door, probably when the new lock was installed, with no footprints leading away into the house. The air inside smelled frowsty and stale.

She turned to the ground-floor windows. On this level, they were only partially barred. 'If I broke that upper pane,' she said, 'I think I could get in by climbing on the lower bars.'

Fletcher looked over the side of the porch, his face pinched with anxiety. 'That's quite a drop. You'd land in the basement area if you fell. I really don't think that's wise.'

'I'm afraid I have to agree with your friend,' a deep voice replied. 'Too dangerous, especially at your age.'

May and Fletcher turned to see a man standing on the porch in the other half of the semi. He was dressed in scruffy clothing, eyeing them with curiosity while smoking a roll-up. His salt-and-pepper beard and short Afro were flecked with white paint.

'I beg your pardon,' May said. The man couldn't be much younger than herself, if at all. The nerve of some people.

He squinted as he took a long drag from his cigarette, then exhaled. 'If I were you, I'd go through the rear garden. More privacy and probably less secure in the back. Most houses are.' His voice was softly accented. West African, maybe.

'Are you the expert on breaking and entering?' May asked. 'Or just a nosy neighbour?'

He smiled, revealing immaculate white teeth. 'A bit of both,' he replied.

May glanced towards the other end of Jilly's house. The building on the opposite side had been extended, closing the gap between it and its neighbour.

'You'd have to go over the fence to get in,' the stranger said, watching May. 'Perhaps you could persuade a friendly neighbour to let you have a go.' He leaned against the wall of his porch, eyes never leaving May's face.

'Are you offering?' May said.

'Are you asking?' he replied.

They stared at each other over the low brick wall separating them. Fletcher fidgeted, looking from May to the stranger as the seconds stretched.

'No, I'm not,' May said at last. 'But thanks for the input.' She grabbed Fletcher's arm and pushed him back towards the motorbike.

The man on the porch smoked and smiled as he watched them go.

CHAPTER THIRTY

YOU REALLY GOT ME

'Who was that?' Fletcher whispered as they stood on the pavement, self-consciously putting on their helmets. The stranger remained on the porch, watching them as he smoked.

'I don't know. The decorator?' May snapped. 'It may surprise you to know that I am not familiar with every single person who lives in the Greater London area.' She mounted the bike in an obvious huff and waited for Fletcher to clamber on behind her. He considered walking back to Greenway on his own, then remembered the journalists waiting outside the house.

Speaking through the helmet mic as May started the engine, he said, 'Do you think that chap has a point? Should we try to get in through the garden? Perhaps she's got the dogs back there.'

'Where the hell do you think I'm going?' May replied, revving the engine, then skidding the bike in a wide turning circle before speeding away so quickly they left a spray of gravel in their wake.

Fletcher held on for dear life. If he didn't know better, he'd think May was showing off.

They drove through the village, turning into Blackheath Grove, then retraced their steps to drive around to Pond Road. May stopped several times to stand on the foot pegs and get her bearings.

'Jilly's garden backs onto the train tracks. We might be able to get in via Pond Road, but I need a satellite image to be certain,' she said. 'Let's go to the shop and see if Bastian can help. He can take a look at the door locks at the same time.'

Fletcher's bum and thighs ached from clenching them so tightly to remain upright on the narrow bike seat. A comfy chair, a hot coffee and a delicious cake sounded like the perfect antidote.

Unfortunately, the bookshop was once again full to overflowing. Fletcher's hopes for a pleasant rest were crushed as they pushed their way through the crowd outside the door. Bastian was standing on a chair beside the front counter, looking around the room then tapping on his phone. He pointed at his watch, then waved May and Fletcher over.

9.58am.

Fletcher's stomach dropped. He'd almost forgotten about the text messages. If Jilly was behind them, then surely there'd be no message when she was away.

'I'm trying to make a note of everyone who's here,' Bastian said, once they were close enough to speak. 'I've given up on serving more drinks. Jilly's not here and I'm out of cups and saucers anyway.' He nodded towards the crowd. Most people were holding a drink in their hand. Fletcher tried not to show his disappointment.

'We need to talk to you,' May said. 'When would be a good time?'

'Once the text shows up, everyone will clear out,' Bastian replied.

Just as he stopped speaking there was a flurry of beeps, pings and buzzes.

The next message had arrived.

Ten minutes later, Fletcher, May and Bastian sat in the empty bookshop at a table in the back.

'That didn't take long,' May said, as the dishwasher thumped and whooshed behind her.

'It's the same every morning at the moment,' Bastian said. 'Absolute mayhem, followed by absolute tranquillity.'

Fletcher looked at the text on his phone.

> Love sought is good but what you're doing is disgusting. Stop sleeping around and just grow old gracefully. MM

'You think this one's for you?' Fletcher asked May.

May shrugged. 'If it is, they're wrong for once. I certainly haven't been sleeping around, unless they count dozing off at the kitchen table.'

'Let's come back to the message in a moment,' Bastian said, sipping his green tea. 'You had something you wanted to talk over?'

May took a deep breath. 'There are a thousand things spinning through my head right now. Do you have a pen and paper?'

It helped May to write things down. The shelves in her library were crowded with journals and ledgers where she kept track of events, things to do and people to kill.

Once Bastian had provided a bit of foolscap and handed over his Montblanc pen, May started her list.

1. Bess and George – missing

'The dogs are missing?' Bastian asked, reading over her shoulder. 'Since when?'

'We think since yesterday,' May said. 'It was a very long, very trying day. I can't be certain, but they didn't touch their afternoon meal which is unusual. None of us recall seeing them from about five o'clock.'

Bastian crossed his arms, a look of concern on his face. 'Right. What else?'

2. Virgilia

'Did you know Jilly's name is Virgilia?' Fletcher said. 'Minty mentioned it. I believe Shakespeare invented the name for *Coriolanus*. That made us think of the text messages and we realised that Jilly was here for most of them.'

Bastian nodded. 'Yes, I believe she was. On Monday, when the first text was sent, she was upstairs cleaning the flat.'

'With her job, she must have keys to most of the houses in Blackheath. She certainly has access to the vicarage,' Fletcher said.

'We went straight to her house,' May said. 'But she's gone away and we couldn't get in. Do you know where she went?'

Bastian shook his head. 'She came in to say she'd be away for a few weeks. She was in a rush and was a bit flustered. It seemed to be a last-minute thing, but she didn't say where she was going.'

May nodded. 'She came to my house and spoke to Minty, saying much the same thing.' She extracted her phone from the capacious Kelly bag and showed Bastian the photos she'd taken. 'Do you know anything about these door locks?'

3. Keyless locks

Bastian raised his eyebrows. 'This is on Jilly's house? That's a very serious lock.' He took out his phone and tapped at the screen a moment. 'Okay, that makes sense. It's made by Oluso Locks. Asa Oluso moved into the other half of Jilly's semi about six months ago. He probably installed them for her.' He whistled. 'This one's called The Porter. They say it's tamper-proof, requires two-step verification, encrypted. You'd need the key tag or a battering ram to get in.'

'Asa Oluso?' Fletcher said. He turned to May. 'That must be the chap who suggested going in through the garden.'

'He's a locksmith?' May asked, intrigued.

'Used to be,' Bastian said. 'He invented these locks, made a fortune, then retired and became an artist.' He tapped on his phone again, then handed it to May. On the screen was a series of all-white canvases.

'This is his work?' she asked. 'Blank canvases? It's been done.' She seemed disappointed.

'Very Malevich,' Fletcher said, examining the screen.

'They're more interesting in person.' Bastian put his phone away. 'He builds up thick layers of colour, then covers them in white paint. Some of the canvases are slashed so the layers are visible. It's all about the unseen, the unspeakable things we keep hidden. You should go take a look.'

'Hmm, maybe more reminiscent of Shimamoto,' Fletcher said. 'What do you think?' He turned to May, but she was miles away, staring at the space where Bastian's phone had been. 'May?'

She looked up at them, then sat back in her chair and

sighed. 'Maybe the garden is the way to go. Do you have access to a satellite image so we can see exactly where Jilly's garden fence lies? I don't want to be climbing over fence after fence trying to find it.'

'Easy-peasy,' Bastian replied, emptying his cup with a final swig then going to get his laptop from the flat.

'Do you think Mrs Lovelace is upstairs?' Fletcher whispered.

May shrugged. 'They were bickering in the kitchen when I was here yesterday, but he still hasn't said anything about her. Referred to her as "a friend" staying with him. It's weird.'

Fletcher cleared his throat. 'Once this is all over, we should go see that artist chap's work. Sounds fascinating.' He looked at May from the corner of his eye while he fiddled with a teaspoon. Would she take the bait?

Apparently not. 'Can you remember where we put the portable stepladder?' she asked.

Fletcher grimaced. 'Are we really going to be scaling fences this afternoon?'

'Don't be silly,' May replied. 'We'll wait for nightfall.'

Nightfall? Christ, it was like living with Lupin sometimes.

May had that look that both thrilled and terrified Fletcher. He knew he was going to be forced to do something he absolutely did not want to do. He also knew that he'd probably love every minute of it.

Bastian returned and opened up Google Earth. They were soon studying an aerial view of Bennett Park.

Fletcher shook his head. 'This technology must be an absolute boon to thieves.'

On the screen was Jilly's back garden, overgrown and with what looked like a dilapidated shed in the corner. Unfortunately, there was no alleyway, just a patchwork of gardens behind the houses on Bennett Park and Pond Road with the train line cutting a swathe through the green. May moved the image this way and that, then pointed at the screen.

'We have to either go in from the train tracks here at the back or go through this house and over one, two, three fences, crossing two rear gardens in the process to get in from the side.' She pursed her lips. The wrinkle between her eyes deepened.

Fletcher was torn between hoping it was too much of a challenge for them, and sad that May might feel defeated by it. 'Let's do it,' he blurted, surprising everyone including himself. He looked at the screen. 'Going in from the tracks seems the most efficient way.' His stomach gurgled in protest. The train tracks were above ground, but sunk into a deep cutting. Getting down to them and up the other bramble-covered side would be no easy feat. He ignored his churning stomach and continued. 'When's the last train? Midnight? If we wait until then it'll make things easier.'

May looked at Fletcher. 'Are you sure? It's a big risk.' She was beaming approval.

'What about this Oluso, Jilly's neighbour?' Fletcher backtracked. 'He seemed interested in helping.'

'No,' she said firmly. 'I'm not asking him for anything.'

'Just a moment,' Bastian interrupted, ever the voice of reason. 'Does no one else have a key card? Surely Jilly gave one to someone for emergencies?'

May nodded with reluctance. 'Minty did say that Betty has a fob or something. We could probably ask her for it.'

'Speak of the Devil,' Bastian said, as the shop bell rang and Betty Danvers walked in.

CHAPTER THIRTY-ONE

PUPPY LOVE

May slumped in a chair in her library, hands shaking with fury. 'I can't believe she wouldn't give us the fob. What did she think we were going to do? Rob the place?'

'Betty does have a point,' Fletcher said gently. 'And she did try to ring Jilly for permission. It's not Betty's fault that Jilly has her phone switched off. Not that Jilly would've given her permission to let us in if she's the guilty party.' He subsided into silence. Stumped by his own reckoning.

May closed her eyes. Speaking slowly, she said, 'Reason and logic are not what's needed at the moment, dear. Read the fucking room.'

'Let's burn her house down,' Minty said with gusto, going to the drinks trolley.

May scowled at her. 'That might feel good in the moment,' she replied. 'But we still wouldn't have the key. Haven't you had enough to drink?'

Minty added a second shot of gin to the glass. 'I was actually making this for you,' she said. '*Was* being the operative word.'

May stared at the fireplace. Betty lived on Blackheath Vale, just around the corner from May. 'Betty said the damn thing is on a hook in her kitchen, "safe and sound". It's so close. I can almost taste it.'

May and Fletcher had returned to Greenway the same way they'd left, whizzing past the journalists on Patsy. The crowd in front of the house had thinned through the afternoon, though a few die-hards remained.

'Do you think they'll camp on the heath?' Minty asked, looking out the window.

'Not allowed,' May replied. 'Though they could sit there on a bench all night if they chose to. Right now, they are the least of my worries. All I care about is Bess and George. Everything points to Jilly being behind these messages.' May counted the points off on her fingers. 'There's the Shakespeare connection with her name. She was around when each text was sent. She has access to houses in the village, including the vicarage, and therefore access to their secrets. She came to the house yesterday when the dogs went missing, and she's suddenly disappeared off the face of the earth.'

'Just a moment,' Fletcher interjected. 'What about the message this morning? We keep ignoring it. How did Jilly send that one?'

May flapped her hands at him. 'Bastian is working on it. I'm sure he'll find the answer. Maybe a timed message on a phone tucked behind a book or hidden in his flat? Who knows? Right now I just want to focus on getting into that bloody house.'

'What did the message say?' Minty asked. Fletcher held out his phone so Minty could squint at the screen. 'Oh!' she said. 'How thrilling. I think this one is about me.'

'Your initials are AM,' May said. 'In case you've forgotten.'

Minty sat down with her drink, stirring it with one finger. 'But most people call me Minty. And, in case *you've* forgotten, I'm the only MM in this house to bump uglies in years.'

Fletcher chortled as May turned to face her mother. 'I beg your pardon,' May said.

'It's a reference to genit—' Fletcher started.

May held up a hand. 'Yes, I can work it out for myself, thank you very much.'

Minty grinned as she sipped her drink, staining the rim of the glass with her coral lipstick.

'You may have a point,' May conceded. 'But how would anyone know about Humphrey?'

'The condom!' Fletcher said. 'Anyone who used the downstairs loo could've seen the condom in the bin.' He made a face. 'And the rubber gloves and tweezers. Good Lord, what must they think you've been doing?'

'Perhaps you should stay in the house today,' May said to Minty. 'Where did Jilly go when she came round yesterday? Did she go into the bathroom or kitchen?'

Fletcher's mouth fell open as he realised where May was going with her questions. 'You don't think?' he said. He looked around the room, as if there were booby traps behind the sofa and landmines under the rugs.

Minty narrowed her eyes in concentration. 'She didn't go into the kitchen,' she said. 'Just stood in the hall for a few moments while we talked.'

'She does have a key to the house,' May said, mouth tense. 'She might've waited until we were asleep to get up to mischief.'

Minty shook her head. 'I was awake until I heard you coming downstairs around six. She didn't come in overnight.'

May relaxed a bit. 'At least that's something. We should still be mindful though. Don't forget Juan's coffee pods.'

'This gin and tonic seems fine,' Minty replied with a wink. 'I'll stick to these this evening. For my own safety.'

After a cautious dinner of eggs and tinned baked beans, Minty decided on an early night.

'Goodnight you two. Don't do anything I wouldn't do,' she said as she left the kitchen.

'That leaves us wide open,' May replied. She turned to Fletcher, who was going through the kitchen pantry, tossing everything into the bin that could possibly have been tampered with for the second time that week. 'I'll do another shop tomorrow,' May said. 'We'll all feel more comfortable when we can eat without fear of being poisoned.'

Fletcher took the container of Horlicks down from the cupboard. He took one look at the malty powder within, then chucked it away and washed his hands at the sink. 'G&T?' he said.

'What a waste,' May replied, nodding towards the rubbish. 'I don't know when Jilly could've possibly doctored the food, but it's probably best to be careful. What an absurd situation.'

Fletcher picked up a lemon, examined it carefully, then tossed it away as well. 'We'll do without the lemon tonight. I can't help but think of Turing's apple.'

May sat at the kitchen table, staring at the full dog bowls. Was Jilly feeding them properly? George had such a sensitive stomach. She couldn't eat just any old dog food. Were they warm enough? Were they getting enough water? Were they afraid?

'Penny for them,' Fletcher said, sitting opposite May with their drinks.

'Just thinking about the dogs.' She rubbed at her eyes.

'We'll get them back.' Fletcher tapped his glass against May's before taking a sip. 'How well do you know Jilly? Any idea where she'd go?'

May shook her head. 'Not really. Her family moved here when she was a baby. From Cockermouth, I believe.'

'Cockermouth?' Fletcher said. 'That sounds like a decent Saturday night.'

May rolled her eyes but couldn't stop herself from smiling. 'You're disgusting,' she said.

'All the best people are,' he replied. 'What's on the menu tonight, Flambeau? A little breaking and entering? Some light larceny?'

'Pretty much,' May said. 'The key fob is on a hook in Betty's kitchen. I'll pick the lock on her front door then nip in and out again before anyone knows the difference. We just need to wait until she's definitely asleep.' She tapped her fingers on the table as she thought it over. 'If I'd planned it better, I would've helped her off to sleep with a little something.'

'What do we do in the meantime?' Fletcher asked. 'Should we try to get some sleep ourselves?'

'That's probably a good idea,' May said. She yawned. 'You go ahead. I don't think I can sleep until this is done.'

'I know what we can do.' Fletcher stood up and walked over to the freezer. 'I've been saving a little something for just such an occasion.'

CHAPTER THIRTY-TWO

IT'S ALL WRONG, BUT IT'S ALL RIGHT

Fletcher made a show of extracting the frosty bottle of Brennivín from the freezer. He opened it with a crackling sound. 'They don't call it a safety seal for nothing,' he said, grabbing shot glasses from the cupboard.

'You don't have any *hákarl* in there, do you?' May asked. She'd tried the Icelandic fermented shark meat once before. Once had been enough.

Fletcher chuckled, remembering May's reaction to the ammonia-scented dish during their time in Reykjavík. *Hákarl* was definitely an acquired taste. One that neither of them had acquired. 'I saw some sardines in the pantry,' he said. 'Just let me know if you start craving something fishy.' He poured them each a generous shot.

'*Skál*,' they said, as they clinked glasses and downed their shots.

May exhaled slowly. 'That takes me right back. If I close my eyes, we could be sitting in that funny little bar on Laugavegur playing chess.'

'What a good idea.' Fletcher jumped up and left the kitchen, reappearing a moment later with the chessboard. He started setting up a game as May refilled their glasses. 'All we need now is a big hairy chap singing Dolly Parton's greatest hits in an Icelandic accent,' he said as he switched on the radio. The Turtles harmonised quietly in the background. 'Not quite the same, but it'll do.'

May laughed. 'That was a fantastic trip. *Skál*. To Dolly.'

As it had always been and would always be, May played white and opened with E4. 'Have you thought more about what you want to do about this Barb story?' she asked.

Fletcher moved to D5. 'Almost constantly. It seems to be the white noise in my head at the moment, though I'm no further forward in deciding how to handle it.' In truth, he wished it would all just go away and things could go back to the way they were before.

May took his pawn. 'You know, things will never be the same again,' she said, as if reading his thoughts. 'Every time Barb writes a new book, this story will resurface.' She locked eyes with him across the chessboard. 'You've lived a double life for a long time. Maybe it's time to just be *you*. All of you. All at the same time, whatever form that takes.'

He moved his queen to take her pawn. May huffed in response and poured more drinks as Fletcher studied her face. He'd been looking at the portrait of Bertie in the rear sitting room that afternoon. It was odd that he'd never noticed how different the two of them were. May took after Minty in so many ways, but she was taller and slimmer than her mother. Bertie had been neither tall nor slim. He'd been a pudding of a man who'd been very lucky indeed to catch the eye of the lithe and lovely Minty.

May moved a knight to C3 and continued, 'You've cut yourself in half for years. For good reasons, I know. Often for your own safety.' She shook her head in disgust at the world. 'We chop ourselves up into little pieces to make us more palatable to everyone else. I was "James's wife" for decades and played the role well, even sacrificing my own identity in the process.' She sighed and looked up at him. 'Surely, we're too old for that shit now.' Drink sometimes made May dogmatic.

Fletcher moved his queen back to D8, still wondering about the identity of her father as he half-listened to her pontificate.

'If we can't be who we really are *now,* then when the hell can we? I say no more chopping ourselves up into pieces to please other people. No more pacifying other people, protecting their fragile egos. If we're too much for someone, that's their problem, not ours. Let's just be *us,* whatever that means and fuck the world.'

'*Skål!* Fuck the world!' Fletcher said, snapping back to attention. He squinted at the board. The pieces seemed to be moving back and forth of their own accord.

May slid a pawn to D4. 'You don't owe anyone anything,' she said. 'Barb doesn't owe anyone anything. Just do whatever the hell you want.'

'What are you going to do?' Fletcher asked. 'The dating app, the vibrator, it seems like you're entering a new stage of life too.'

May looked at him, perplexed. 'Vibrator? What on earth are you talking about?'

'I heard it,' he said. 'In your bedroom.'

May stared at him as if trying to decipher a foreign language. Then her face broke into a smile. 'You numpty,' she said, starting to laugh. 'You heard me using my new face shaver.' She shook her head. 'What are you like? Not that I'm opposed to vibrators, now that you mention it. Might be a good idea.'

Fletcher moved a knight to C6. 'And the dating app?'

She shrugged. 'I see you and Sparks together and I'd like a bit of that. Nothing serious, mind. I have no plans to be anyone's wife ever again, but it would be nice to feel desired at least one more time before I die.' She moved a knight to F3.

'You're Minty's child. If that's anything to go by, you've got decades of shagging ahead of you.' Who could Minty have slept with that she wouldn't have wanted to marry? Should he share this new mystery with May?

'Don't,' May replied. 'I don't even want to hear the words "Minty" and "shagging" in the same sentence.'

He'd keep it to himself a bit longer.

'Did you kill James?' Fletcher asked, surprising them both.

May looked at him, suddenly sober. 'No. No, I didn't. I've told you that already. What makes you ask again?'

Fletcher looked at the board, then back at May. 'It's the glass eye in the library. I never noticed it before, but Minty pointed it out. It's James's eye, isn't it?' He fiddled with a bishop before placing it on G4, as he waited for May to respond.

'Of course, it would be Minty who noticed.' She moved her pawn to D5. 'Yes, it's James's eye.' Fletcher gasped. 'His *old* eye,' she clarified. 'It's the glass eye he wore when we first met. He replaced it with an acrylic one years ago.' She sat back in the chair. 'It sounds silly but, when he looked at me with that eye, he still loved me. With that eye he saw a woman he admired, a woman he *desired*. I guess I wanted to hold on to that feeling in some small way.'

'I'm sorry,' Fletcher said, immediately contrite. 'I should've known better. You're not silly at all. Let's forget I said anything.' He moved his knight to E5.

May used her knight to take his. 'James has been on my mind,' she admitted. 'I received the divorce papers from him this morning. It's really happening. We still have all the financial mess to sort out, which will probably take ages. The fool wants me to sell Greenway and split the profits fifty–fifty.'

Fletcher was just moving his bishop to take May's queen, when he was stopped in his tracks. 'What? That's absurd.

Surely he doesn't have any claim on the house?' He took her queen. 'Check,' he mumbled, before placing a pawn on C6.

May took his pawn, putting her own in its place. 'No, he'll never get his hands on Greenway. The man's a moron for even suggesting it. The trust is wrapped up tighter than a gnat's arsehole. That's not what bothers me. The letter got me thinking about who'll live here when I'm gone. It has to be a Morrigan, or the house goes to Greenwich Council.'

Fletcher moved his queen to C7. 'You do have family,' he said. 'Maybe it's time to build some bridges.'

'Why does *The Bridge on the River Kwai* immediately spring to mind?' she replied, using her pawn to take his from B7.

He grunted, then moved his queen to D8. 'Surely it wouldn't be that bad. You were very close once and look at all the progress you've made with Minty. I haven't heard her ask you to kill her all day today.'

May moved her knight to F7. 'Checkmate,' she said.

CHAPTER THIRTY-THREE

THE NIGHT HAS A THOUSAND EYES

Six games and three shots of Brennivín later, it was 3am and they were ready to do some trespassing.

'Don't wear the black cashmere this time,' May said. 'You'll just get upset if it's damaged. We need to look normal.'

'How's this?' Fletcher asked, pulling a balaclava over his face.

'No, no, no. We need to look as if we're out for an innocent stroll. Let's take the dogs as cover.' She picked up the leads from their hook beside the door, then froze. 'Oh! Oh, no. I'd forgotten.' Her face crumpled.

Fletcher hadn't seen May cry in years. She could be vulnerable. She could be sad, but May Morrigan rarely cried.

He moved to put his arms around her but May held up a hand to stop him. Fletcher watched as her iron will reasserted itself, rising from her feet, up through her spine, lifting her chin, until she was composed once more.

'We don't have time for that,' she said. 'Let's get this done.'

Outside Greenway, they carefully locked the door behind them and started up the path. The streetlight in front of the house was still broken, creating a deeper darkness in the front garden than usual. Fletcher instinctively looked from side to side as they walked away from the safety of the house. The heath stretched before them, dotted with lamp posts, wrapped in silence. Not a single soul was out.

New York may be the city that doesn't sleep, but London *sleeps*. In fact, London passes right out. There are a few magical hours in the very early morning when one could walk across Tower Bridge undisturbed. It can be enchanting when there's not a killer lurking about. At that moment, Fletcher felt less enchanted, more terrified.

'Are you sure this is a good idea?' he whispered.

'We can always climb the train cutting if you prefer,' May said.

'Righto. Crack on then.' He pulled his jacket tighter and they set off for Blackheath Vale and Betty's home.

As they passed The Cretin's house next door to Greenway, May took out her phone and tapped at the screen. The modern home blazed into life as every light was switched on. Through the floor-to-ceiling windows, they saw Geoffrey's silhouette spring out of bed and stumble around the room.

Fletcher looked at May. 'The Abode app,' she explained. 'Geoffrey gave me his password for the alarm when I collected his post for him. He uses the same password for everything.'

They stood on the pavement watching Geoffrey, like a shadow puppet against the house's sheer curtains, moving from room to room switching off each light while swearing loud enough to be heard out on the pavement.

'Sometimes, if I can't sleep, I come out here and do this,' May said. 'It always makes me feel better.'

Once the final light had been extinguished, they turned and continued towards Blackheath Vale. 'You're evil,' Fletcher whispered with a grin. 'You do know that?'

'It's one of my favourite qualities,' May replied, tapping her phone screen again. The path behind them was flooded with light. They could hear Geoffrey's bellow of frustration from the other end of the street.

In the eerie pre-dawn quiet, their footsteps seemed unnaturally loud. Fletcher felt as if they should be carefully tip-toeing, rather than walking in such a normal way at that ungodly hour, shoes tapping and grating as they went. He jumped as a fox called out somewhere on the heath. It sounded very much like a woman screaming.

They were at the corner of Blackheath Vale when someone barrelled out of the darkness right into them from the other direction.

Betty Danvers.

'You almost gave me a heart attack,' Betty said, grasping her chest and breathing loudly.

'What on earth are you doing out at this hour?' May asked, while Fletcher leaned on a nearby garden wall to catch his breath and calm his nerves. When Betty appeared, he'd shrieked in a way that put the fox on the heath to shame.

'I often walk at night,' Betty said. 'Since Chester died, I've had terrible insomnia. The bed just feels too empty, I'm sure you understand.' She looked at May. 'Sometimes it helps to take a turn around the heath. What are you two doing out at this hour? Can't you sleep?'

'The alarm at the bookshop went off,' May said. 'I was going to make sure it was just a false alarm.'

Fletcher raised his eyebrows, impressed by the quick lie. 'That's right,' he added, pulling himself together and going to stand beside May. 'I came along to help.'

'Won't Bastian handle it?' Betty asked, looking across the heath to the shop. 'It seems quiet now.'

'Bastian's away this evening,' May replied. 'And it's a silent alarm. I was notified on my phone. It's probably nothing, but I know I won't be able to sleep until I'm sure.'

'That's right,' Fletcher said. 'Me neither.' May elbowed him in the ribs.

'I won't keep you then,' Betty replied, stepping aside.

May and Fletcher said goodnight then started off across the heath towards Burgos Books.

May lifted her phone to her ear and spoke loudly as they walked away. 'Hello, Bastian? I'm just going to check it out now. No, don't worry...' She whispered through gritted teeth, 'Is she still standing there?'

Fletcher turned and waved. 'Yep,' he said. 'She's going to watch us all the way to the shop. I guess we're not getting that key tonight.'

'Don't worry about that,' May said. 'I've got another idea.'

'I bet you do,' Fletcher replied slowly. 'I just bet you do.'

CHAPTER THIRTY-FOUR

PAPA'S GOT A BRAND NEW BAG

After far too little sleep, Fletcher woke up on Easter morning certain that he knew the identity of May's father: Mordecai Page. It had come to him in a dream, but it made perfect sense. Minty had said more than once how successful Mordecai had been with the ladies of Blackheath back in the day. Was it such a stretch to suggest that Minty might've taken her turn on the Hobby Horse with disastrous consequences?

Fletcher knew that Mordecai had been a POW. Had Minty married Bertie because she'd thought Mordecai was dead? Had she loved him? The thought revolted Fletcher. He couldn't bring himself to believe it, though it had been a long time ago and he knew that war changed people.

Still, Minty and Mordecai in love? Never. Even if they'd spent some time together, enough to get pregnant, he couldn't imagine Minty marrying the man by choice.

Should he take these thoughts to May? No, he needed proof.

He could ask Minty, but she was obviously uncomfortable with the subject. Their chat over the Horlicks had been an anomaly. How could he prove the theory without Minty's confirmation?

DNA.

Fletcher sat up in bed. That's what he needed. If he could get a sample of Mordecai's DNA, he could send it off to be analysed. Once he knew for sure, he'd speak to May.

Fletcher picked up his phone from the bedside cabinet and started tapping. He knew just the person to help him.

CHAPTER THIRTY-FIVE

ONE FINE DAY

As the bells of St Julian's rang out over the heath, the residents of Greenway gathered for breakfast.

'You two look rough as old boots,' Minty said as she switched on the kettle.

'Thank you, Mother dear,' May replied. 'It was a late night.'

Fletcher, at the Aga frying eggs, grunted in agreement.

Minty had been up and dressed for hours, taking special care as they'd all be taking part in the day's celebrations. May's bookshop had a stall at the church's Easter fête on the heath, so Minty wanted to look her best. There was bound to be a handsome granddad or two in attendance.

'Did you get the key thingy?' Minty asked. She felt marvellous. Maybe she was ageing backwards. These two old fogeys would have to learn to keep up.

May rubbed her eyes and yawned. 'Not yet,' she said. 'But Betty will be on the heath today. That's when we'll get into her house and get the fob.' She scrolled through her phone, checking her messages. 'During the egg hunt would be the best time. She won't want to miss that.' May sagged in her chair. 'Bastian hasn't seen any ads that might be Bess or George online. I almost hoped he'd found something. At least it would be progress, of a sort.'

She looked so haggard. May really should've had children. She already worried like an overprotective mother.

'I'm sure the dogs are fine,' Minty said. 'If someone is planning to sell them, they'll be caring for them, keeping them healthy.'

'I hope you're right,' May replied.

At the Aga, Fletcher remained unusually silent.

CHAPTER THIRTY-SIX

SINNERMAN

After breakfast, Fletcher dressed quickly in his new baby-blue suit then announced that he was popping into the village. He decided to leave the sling at home, too distinctive, and his shoulder was feeling much better. Once out of sight of Greenway, he took the 89 bus to Lewisham. Fletcher's online search for Mordecai's address had been fruitless. Apart from a brief mention on the St Julian's website, there was no trace of Mordecai Page online at all.

Then Fletcher remembered the old BT phone book May kept in the library. Flicking through the tissue-thin pages, he found a 'Page, Mordecai M' who lived at 71 Limes Grove in Lewisham. How many Mordecai Pages could there be in southeast London? Fletcher just hoped he hadn't moved house before he died.

Getting off the bus at the clocktower, Fletcher strolled through the market. Lewisham was always a stimulating place to visit. Just a mile from Blackheath Village, its busy urban edge provided a sharp contrast to the Arcadian calm of Blackheath Village. He stopped to buy some buns from Suzy at the Bluebird. If needed, they would provide his excuse for going into Lewisham. Removing the extra bun he'd purchased for immediate gratification, he dawdled at the market stalls, admiring the artichokes and chicory and spring greens on display, delaying what he'd gone there to do. Whenever Fletcher visited the market, he always wondered why he didn't go there more often. There were always items to discover and bargains to be had.

Just before the library, Fletcher turned left onto Limes Grove. He counted off the numbers until he arrived in front of number 71. It was a small Victorian terraced house, not in the best condition, but cared for in a 'make do and mend' sort of way. He walked past the house to the end of the street, then turned and walked back again, trying to build up his nerve.

Taking a deep breath, he marched up to the front door and knocked. There was no answer. Hopefully, that was a good sign. Trying to peep in through the front windows, he found the blinds were all drawn down without a gap. He'd been hoping to see something to confirm that Mordecai had indeed still been living there, otherwise Fletcher would be breaking into a stranger's house for no reason.

He glanced around the quiet street then knocked again, just to be certain. The door looked to be the original Victorian with two decorative stained-glass panels. Fletcher knew a thing or two about stained glass. He examined each panel closely. Using his good hand, he pushed the glass on the right side and the pane sagged inwards, the leading had deteriorated and weakened over time. He pushed harder and heard a crack, cringing at the damage he was causing. In his anxious state, the noise sounded like a gunshot, causing him to look frantically up and down the street. The coast was still clear.

It's now or never, he thought, pushing harder still until the old pane started to give way, dropping coloured glass onto the mat inside. Just a bit more and he'd be able to reach inside and unlatch the door.

'Fletcher? I thought that was you,' a voice said behind him.

Fletcher jumped, then turned to see Danny Fox standing on the pavement.

'What are you doing?' Danny asked, his young face crinkled with confusion as he looked at Fletcher's hand which was halfway through the glass panel. Then his face cleared. 'Is this to do with Mr Page's death? Do you and May think it's suspicious?'

Danny Fox had assisted May and Fletcher in finding a young girl who'd disappeared a few months previously. He possessed a sharp mind, which had come in handy during his brief career as a journalist. Fox had recently switched to writing a true crime account of the missing girl's case, which had turned out to be much bigger than they had ever imagined.

'Danny, how nice to see you,' Fletcher said, awkwardly turning with his hand still lodged in the window. He didn't want to remove it too quickly. A nasty cut would not be welcome, especially while wearing his new suit. He decided to play off the situation as casually as possible. 'I'm a bit busy at the moment,' he said. 'But it would be lovely to catch up soon.'

Fox walked up the short, tiled path to the house's tiny porch. 'Go ahead,' he said. 'I'll keep a lookout.' He turned his back to Fletcher to obstruct the view of anyone who might be watching.

Fletcher hesitated.

'Go on,' Fox encouraged. 'You're obviously trying to break into the place. I live at number 67; I know who lives here.'

Danny Fox had proved a formidable ally in the past. Fletcher quickly made up his mind and pushed the glass panel until it completely gave way, then he slipped his hand through the gap and released the latch. A moment later, he and Fox were both standing on the mat inside Mordecai Page's deserted house.

'So,' Fox said, 'what are we looking for?'

'I'm not sure,' Fletcher lied. 'I just wanted to have a look around the place.' He headed towards the stairs. The bathroom was the obvious location for what he needed. 'You have a look down here and see if you can find anything suspicious,' he said to Fox.

Fletcher's old friend, Dr Satoshi Akashi at the Strangeways Research Lab in Cambridge, had said that a DNA test could be conducted using DNA extracted from hair, nail clippings, or a recently used toothbrush. Fletcher and Satoshi had met when they'd both been readers at Cambridge. They'd bonded over a shared love of good food, which had been thin on the ground in Cambridge in the seventies. Fletcher owed his admirable knife skills to Satoshi's calm patience.

When Fletcher had put forth his query, Satoshi had been delighted to be of assistance. The lab had some new equipment and he looked forward to any opportunity to test it. Satoshi's speciality was genetic epidemiology, so confirming paternity would be child's play. If Fletcher could get the samples to him that morning, he'd have the CODIS Core Loci STR profile in just a few hours. He assured Fletcher that this would definitely either confirm or deny paternity.

Upstairs in Mordecai's house, Fletcher looked around the small landing. The house was surprisingly tidy, almost bare. He'd been expecting something more cave-like, more malodorous. He sniffed the air, which was positively fresh. Then he remembered that Mordecai had been in the British army. The clean surfaces, compulsive order, and sharp bed corners made sense. The concern was that this cleanliness meant there would be no nail clippings to be found or strands of hair tangled in a greasy comb by the bathroom sink.

Fletcher began his search. As feared, the tiny bedroom was spotless. In the wardrobe, amongst the neatly folded clothing on a shelf, he found a photo album. Flipping through the brittle pages, he saw a number of photos of Mordecai as a young man in uniform. Surprisingly handsome and virile-looking, Fletcher felt aggrieved at what war had done to so much potential. If that dashing young man was May's father, then perhaps the angry, lascivious old git they'd known wasn't such a travesty.

At the back of the album was a photo of a group of young people dressed for dancing. Fletcher recognised the alligator painted on the wall behind them from the Blackheath caves. He scanned the group, easily spotting Mordecai grinning at the camera in the centre of the crowd. There beside him, her arms thrown around the shoulders of him and another soldier, was a lovely, beaming Minty. Fletcher carefully removed the photo – Mordecai wasn't going to miss it – and tucked it into his blazer pocket.

He moved on to the bathroom. The tiles and fittings were obviously old, but the room was spick and span. No hair left in the comb inside the medicine cabinet, but there was Mordecai's toothbrush in the glass on the shelf. Fletcher wrapped some loo roll around his hand before picking up the toothbrush. He remembered Mordecai's chronic halitosis and feared that the toothbrush hadn't been used recently enough for the DNA test. He hesitantly sniffed the bristles, recoiling in disgust. It would have to do.

Downstairs, Fox was looking through the few books on the shelves in the sitting room. 'It feels like he's only just moved into the place,' he said. 'There's so little here. Did you find anything useful upstairs?'

'Not really,' Fletcher said, very much aware of the photo and the toothbrush wrapped in loo roll tucked in his pocket. 'Have you seen any tape down here?' Now that the job was done, he couldn't wait to get out of the house, send the samples off to Satoshi and resume life as normal.

'Tape?' Fox asked.

'Duct tape, masking tape, anything like that?' Fletcher walked into the kitchen and started opening drawers. He found a roll of duct tape in a drawer full of carefully organised tools.

After mending the broken panel as best they could with the tape, Fletcher and Fox left the house, pulling the door shut behind them.

'Are you going to tell me what that was all about?' Fox asked.

Fletcher thought about it for a moment. 'No,' he replied. 'I'm afraid not.'

Fox smiled, then nodded. 'If you change your mind, you know where to find me,' he said, before strolling away up Limes Grove towards the High Street.

CHAPTER THIRTY-SEVEN

DEVIL WITH A BLUE DRESS ON

Warm sunshine and a fresh breeze created the perfect weather for the St Julian's Easter fête. So many times in the past the fair had been forced to move indoors due to rain, with stands squashed into the crypt and down the aisles of the nave. Those were soggy, subdued affairs. Nothing like the glorious, cheerful spring they were experiencing.

Fletcher was wearing a light-blue suit, set off by sparkling gold earrings, looking very dapper in a straw boater. He'd left his sling at home, saying that it ruined the line of the suit, and hovered around the Burgos Books stall with a glass of Pimms, charming everyone who came to browse. Minty, wearing a pair of enormous sunglasses, established herself on Bastian's tall stool, dragged onto the heath for that purpose. She sat at the front of their small marquee gazing out at the masses, rewarding the lucky few with a smile, while earwigging on every conversation within hearing distance.

May had wandered over to the drinks stall where Minty watched a very handsome man come up behind May and say something that made her scowl. Minty tutted. 'You're never going to get a man with a face like a slapped arse,' she grumbled.

'Did you say something, Minty?' Bastian was helping a punter choose a murder mystery from the stacks of Agatha Christie paperbacks.

Minty shook her head as she continued to watch her daughter. May still had a decent figure. She looked particularly lovely in the turquoise dress she'd chosen that day. Good legs too. Was that a smile? Perhaps all was not lost.

'Fletcher?' She motioned for him to come to her. 'Who's that man talking to May?'

Fletcher adjusted his hat as he looked to where Minty was brazenly pointing. 'I think that's Jilly's neighbour, the artist. Asa something. He cleans up nicely. That's a very well-tailored shirt. Do you think May needs to be rescued?'

At that moment, May actually threw back her head in laughter. Minty and Fletcher looked at each other in surprise.

'I think she's doing just fine,' Minty replied.

As the morning wore on, the crowds increased in the lead-up to the big event, the Easter egg hunt. Father David was there wearing white vestments trimmed in gold for the occasion, putting on a brave face for the parish and accepting condolences. He looked exhausted but was better off surrounded by the warmth and care of his congregation, than home alone consoling himself with a bottle of whisky.

Minty shuffled her stool bit by bit to remain in the shade, as the sun miraculously continued to shine. From her perch, she watched the families enjoying their day out, the teenagers dragged along and suffering through it, young couples browsing the stalls hand in hand, delighting in each other's company. It was the older couples who gave her a pang of regret. Even though it had been almost seventy years, with one husband and many lovers in between, it was her darling who came to mind when she saw the elderly women holding hands with their partners.

Minty could imagine him as an old man, still bright-eyed, still curious about the world. She had no doubt that, if things had gone differently, they would still be together. She wasn't naive and knew that they would've gone through tough times, but he was her home. They could have weathered any storm together. How would her life have been different if she'd spent it with him? How would May have been different if he had raised her?

It was too painful to travel very far down that rabbit hole. Minty reeled herself back to the safety of her happiest memories.

They had often walked on the heath. He'd kissed her under that lamp post. And that one. And that one. Her father would turn the porch light at Greenway off and on, off and on, to signal to Minty to come home, but they would just stroll over to another part of the heath, out of sight.

It was hard to believe so much time had passed. In many ways, Minty felt exactly the same as she did then. That young woman still breathed inside the current one, stacked together with all the other versions of Minty in between, like Russian dolls. Young Minty had had hopes and dreams, love and desire. Now, this Minty just wanted to rest. She'd carried the weight of all those other versions of herself for years. Memories upon memories, pain upon pain. It was time to throw off this tired, old body and give herself to peace.

She scanned the crowd for May, searching for the turquoise dress, finally spotting her and Fletcher huddled together over by the church. May raised her head and looked around until her eyes rested on someone out on the heath, then she and Fletcher turned towards the church. Minty tried to see who May had been looking at, but the egg hunt was about to start, so that area of the heath was full of parents, children and church volunteers.

Betty caught Minty's eye, smiled and waved. She raised a hand in response, then looked back to where May and Fletcher had been standing, but both of them had disappeared.

CHAPTER THIRTY-EIGHT

DEM DRY BONES

The crypt was buzzing with people when May and Fletcher came down the stairs. Women were queueing for the loos with children complaining loudly about the wait. Volunteers were working in the kitchen, ferrying biscuits and jugs of milk to the stall out on the heath, warming scones and Betty's hot cross buns in the oven for the afternoon teas and chopping fruit and mint for the endless glasses of Pimms. It smelled wonderful.

May pulled Fletcher into the utility room and shut the door. She took a doorstop from a shelf and wedged it underneath. 'That'll buy us some time,' she said, before moving to the wall that opened into the Blackheath caves.

'What's happening?' Fletcher asked, eyes irresistibly going to the spot where Mordecai had gasped his last. Was that sad old man really May's father? 'You said we were going to get some scones.'

May slid the wall back and started to push the heavy door open to the tunnels. 'We're going to get that fob from Betty's house,' she replied, dusting off her hands then extracting two torches from her handbag. 'I picked these up when I went to the shops this morning. I'm afraid we'll have to go via the ossuary this time, for the sake of speed.'

Fletcher took one of the torches, scowled at it, flicked it on and off again. He was sulking about the lack of scones, working himself up into a tizzy before even entering the caverns.

'Come on,' May said, ignoring his mood. 'Betty's busy with the egg hunt, but that won't take all afternoon.'

He reluctantly shuffled in beside her as she slid the wall back into place. 'This is a new suit,' he said as they switched on the torches and set off. 'I do *not* want it damaged.'

May, out in front, tutted in response.

'Wait, did you say *ossuary*?' Fletcher asked.

May kept walking. 'Just close your eyes and hold my hand if you need to. It's much faster this way.'

She took a narrow tunnel that led off to the right and continued on. The ceiling was lower here and the walls closer. She could hear Fletcher's sigh of resignation behind her. At the next turning, May braced herself for his reaction.

'You have got to be joking!' he said, skidding to a stop. The narrow pathway stretching in front of them was lined with human bones on both sides, floor-to-head height. Femurs and tibias stacked like kindling in endless piles. Skulls perched on top and embedded in the stacks to form crosses or diamonds, creating ranks of macabre faces gazing out into the darkness.

'Who were these people?' Fletcher whispered, looking around in awe.

Though May had been in the ossuary many times, she still found the sheer number of skeletons astonishing. 'The great and good of Blackheath,' she replied. 'I'm sure more than a few of my ancestors are in pieces here somewhere. The catacombs are much older than the church, going back to the Middle Ages.'

Fletcher swallowed and remained stationary, shining his

torch along the bones arranged in weirdly decorative designs. 'Why are there so many of them?'

'The Black Death,' May replied. 'The heath was used for mass graves, plague pits. A lot of the dead are from that time.'

He pulled his shirt up to cover his mouth and nose. 'The plague?! For God's sake, let's keep going. I don't want to stay here any longer than necessary.' The light from their torches danced against the bones, casting shadows in the eye sockets of the skulls that seemed to follow their conversation.

May shook her head and set off again. The bones created a narrow pathway through a much larger cavern. At points, one could look over the tops of the stacks and see them extending for ten or twelve feet to the chalk walls of the cave. Along the path they were arranged meticulously with femurs, tibias and humeri grouped together then carefully arranged, joints outwards, creating a textured tile effect. Behind this deep wall of bone, the rest of the skeletons were tossed willy-nilly. If one stopped and peered closely, it was possible to identify a pelvis here, a ribcage there, perhaps a clavicle or some vertebrae, a lower jaw still full of teeth. The ossuary was a place of extreme cognitive dissonance, where the dead were both revered and treated like landfill.

In a few moments, they'd passed through the catacombs and arrived in the main chamber with its animal decorations on the walls. May wasted no time and continued on to the tunnel that led to Greenway's cellar.

'We'll go up through the house, then out the back way to Betty's. After that, we'll go straight to Jilly's and see what's what,' she said, glancing at Fletcher who was huffing and puffing behind her. He was cradling his sore arm with his other hand, his torchlight bobbing against the tunnel wall. May stopped. 'Are you going to be okay?' she said. 'Why don't you wait in the house. I won't be ten minutes at Betty's.'

'No.' Fletcher shook his head. 'I'm coming with you. You need a lookout. I'll just take a minute to catch my breath and take another painkiller once we're inside. You're not doing this alone.'

In Greenway's kitchen, he sat on a chair, swiping at the sleeves of his blazer. 'That bloody chalk-dust is a nightmare. I wish you'd warned me about this little adventure. I would've dressed accordingly.'

May handed him two tablets and a glass of water. 'The whole point was to be inconspicuous. Turning up to the Easter fête in a hard hat and dungarees would not have been subtle.'

Fletcher swallowed the tablets before responding. 'As if I own a hard hat and dungarees...' His voice trailed off and his eyes glazed over.

'Before you start planning your next soirée with Sparks,' May said, 'we need to get going. We've got a house to burgle.'

CHAPTER THIRTY-NINE

IT HAD TO BE YOU

'Have you seen Fletcher?' Bastian asked. 'Someone's asking about art books. I could use his expertise.'

Minty shook her head. 'He and May were over by the church a moment ago.' She checked the crowd but couldn't spot May's bright dress or Fletcher's boater anywhere. Where had they got to?

'I thought you were going to watch the shop.' Bastian was speaking to a tall young woman who'd wandered over to the stall. Minty leaned back to hear their conversation more clearly.

'It was boring,' the woman said. 'Everyone is out here.' There was a distinct whine to her voice. Was this the mysterious Mrs Lovelace?

Bastian was obviously not pleased with her answer. 'Did you at least lock up?'

The woman's silence was answer enough.

'Oh, for God's sake,' Bastian said. 'Stay here. *I'll* go lock up.'

Minty turned and smiled at the young woman. 'Hello,' Minty said. 'Are you helping out in the shop?'

'You could say that.' She had long, dark hair and blue eyes.

A pretty little thing. She came over to Minty and held out her hand. 'I'm Erika.'

'Erika?' Minty said. 'You must be Bastian's wife.'

Erika laughed. 'News travels fast around here.'

Behind the dark glasses, Minty looked Erika up and down. She looked to be in her early twenties, simply but expensively dressed in a cotton sundress and sandals, gold hoops in her ears and a tote bag over one arm.

'We may be in London,' Minty said. 'But Blackheath is a village. The bush telegraph is very efficient.'

Erika just smiled.

Bastian returned, sweaty and cross.

'I've just met your lovely bride,' Minty said. 'We should celebrate.'

'My what?' He looked from Minty to Erika, then closed his eyes and took a deep breath. 'Erika is my daughter,' he said, opening his eyes. 'She obviously has a very odd sense of humour.'

Erika laughed, then turned to Minty. 'Bastian is ashamed of me, you see. He only found out that he had a daughter a few weeks ago. I think he preferred it when I didn't exist.'

'That's not true,' Bastian said. 'It's just going to take a little time to adjust. Erika is staying with me for a while, so we can get to know each other.'

How delightfully scandalous!

'That definitely calls for a celebration,' Minty said, taking Erika's hand. 'We can have one of those American-style baby showers, "It's a girl!", but with lots of booze. And maybe a stripper.'

Erika laughed again and seemed delighted with the idea. Bastian grimaced, but looked pleased to see Erika's smile. Minty would soon win him over to the idea.

A whistle blew and the much anticipated egg hunt began.

Children raced around the church and the heath, shouting with excitement every time a brightly coloured egg was found. Anxious parents stood beside the road in clumps, corralling them back towards the fête when the little ones veered too near to the traffic. Hopped-up on chocolate and sweets, the children were virtually feral, running in all directions, eyes glazed with egg lust.

'I don't miss those days.' Betty Danvers had come to stand beside Minty and Erika. Bastian had returned to his stacks. 'I feel tired just watching them,' Betty said, nodding at two parents chasing after a particularly nimble toddler.

Minty introduced Erika to Betty, taking great pleasure in Betty's obvious surprise. Minty was revelling in being the first to know such a prize bit of gossip.

A noisy fight broke out between two children over a hot-pink Easter egg. Tiny fists were flying as the parents tried to separate them, but it was pretty brutal. The smallest child kicked out and screamed like a wounded bull as he was dragged away.

'Good Lord,' Minty said. 'I think I preferred it when children were seen and not heard.'

'My Mary would never have behaved like that,' Betty said. 'That's what comes from a lack of discipline. Parents these days are too afraid to give their children a smack when they need one.'

Minty looked at Betty in surprise. 'Did you smack Mary?' For all of Bertie's faults, he never hit the children. That was something they agreed upon.

'Mary was a lovely child,' Betty replied, 'but they will try to rebel. I remember at fourteen when she cut her hair short without Chester's permission. Oh, she got a smack then, believe me. Silly thing should've known better.' Betty shook her head, smiling, as if recalling a fond memory.

'Could she not choose her own hairstyle at that age?' Erika asked.

Betty frowned. 'Of course not, she was still living under our roof.'

'I see.' Minty was glad Erika was standing beside her. Betty seemed suddenly furious. Her face had gone a blotchy red and she was breathing hard.

'I think I'll go home for a little lie-down,' Betty said without looking at Minty or Erika. She stomped off across the heath, elbowing people out of her way as she went.

Erika raised both eyebrows. 'Is everyone like that around here?'

'No,' Minty replied as she watched Betty go. 'I think Betty Danvers may be in a class of her own.'

She scanned the fair searching for May and Fletcher again. Where had they gone? Then Minty had a horrible thought, had they gone to break into Betty's for that bloody key thingy?

She checked Betty's progress to see that she was already halfway across the heath. Minty needed to do something, and fast.

CHAPTER FORTY

NOWHERE TO RUN

Fletcher had never been to Betty's place before. The little terraced house looked like an illustration from a child's picture book, something quintessentially English by someone like Shirley Hughes or Judith Kerr. The well-kept front garden was blooming with daffodils and irises, with a flowering clematis climbing around the tiny porch. The tiled path was scrubbed, the hedges trimmed and the gleaming windows, showing floral curtains and lacy white sheers within, reflected the bright rays of spring sunlight. Fletcher imagined patchwork quilts, pots of tea and a comfy reading chair within, plus a fat cat sunning itself in a warm kitchen as an old-fashioned kettle whistled on the hob.

For the sake of anyone who might see them from the surrounding houses, May banged the polished brass knocker a few times. When there was no answer, she raised her voice slightly and said to Fletcher, 'I'll have to use my key,' then slipped the picks from her handbag and started working on the lock.

'Hurry up,' Fletcher hissed, looking around the empty street. The sounds of the fête could be heard in the distance. He surreptitiously checked his phone, though there was no way Satoshi would have the results yet. He'd texted Fletcher to say that he'd received the samples just before they'd entered the church.

'Keep your hair on,' May said, as the lock made a satisfying clunk. 'Betty will be away for another hour at least.'

She pushed the door open to reveal a small hallway crowded with coats and shoes, stairs on the right side leading up to the first floor. Yanking Fletcher inside, May shut the door behind them. The smell was the first thing they noticed, rotting rubbish laced heavily with vinegar. Then it was the hall floor, littered with bits of dried mud and dead leaves. Dust bunnies congregating in grey clumps in the corners. It was a harsh contrast to the exterior perfection.

May stepped forward, tentatively sniffing the air, and opened the door on their left. It revealed a small sitting room awash with newspapers piled onto every surface and scattered over the floor. Dirty mugs crowded the top of a small table and lined the floor beside the sofa.

'This isn't just a bit messy, it's properly pathological,' Fletcher said, squeezing his arms closer to his body, trying not to touch anything. 'Looks like Betty's been putting on a brave face, but struggling behind closed doors, poor old thing.'

May knew only too well what that was like.

The kitchen was even worse than the sitting room, with mouldy dishes and crusty baking pans overflowing the sink onto the countertops and windowsill. The oven door hung open, revealing burned buns languishing inside. A soggy mountain of used teabags beside the sink had created a brown waterfall of stains down the front of the lower cabinets. The stench was overwhelming. Fletcher recoiled, covering his nose with his handkerchief.

'Dear God, I ate one of her hot cross buns this morning.' He retched dramatically.

'Don't you dare vomit,' May said. 'Go into the hall if you can't handle it in here.'

Beside the bin was a box that had once held a cheap set of bowls and plates. The bin itself was full to the top with soiled paper plates, burned buns and mucky plastic cutlery.

Betty had bought new dishes instead of washing the dirty ones, then just gave up altogether and switched to paper plates. It looked like she'd been living on ready meals for months. May shook her head in disbelief. She gazed around the manky room. 'My goodness, I guess one never knows what others are dealing with at home.'

Checking behind the kitchen door, she found key hooks but no keys. May raised her voice so Fletcher could hear her. 'Do you see keys anywhere?' she asked, searching the floor. 'I'm afraid this was a wasted housebreaking,' she said, shoving burned baking parchment out of the way with her foot. 'I don't know how we're going to find the key fob in this mess.'

'Thank God for that,' Fletcher said, handkerchief clamped over his mouth and nose. 'Let's get the hell out of here.' He brushed at the sleeves of his jacket and was almost at the front door when a shadow appeared on the door's stained glass, along with the sound of jangling keys.

'Bugger, bugger, bugger,' he whispered, backtracking for the kitchen. May bumped into him, saw the figure on the porch, then opened the nearest door and shoved Fletcher through it. She followed, crowding him into the small space, gripping the big Kelly bag against her chest. They found themselves engulfed in a strong scent of pickles.

May managed to squeeze the door shut behind them just as the front door banged open. They stood like statues in the darkness of the cupboard under the stairs, barely breathing, and listened as Betty entered in what sounded like an angry huff. She stomped up and down the hallway, only inches away.

Fletcher was fuming. How dare May put him in such an awkward situation. How were they ever going to get out of that wretched house? Damn May and her constant meddling.

They were stuck in that cramped, dusty space for God knew how long. The scent of vinegar was overwhelming. A tickle started in the depths of one nostril. Christ, no. Not now. Fletcher pressed his hanky tighter over his face, pinching the bridge of his nose. Hold it in. Hold it in.

As his eyes started to adjust to the darkness, he made out May's silhouette pressed against the cupboard door, eye to a small crack, trying to keep watch on Betty. Fletcher could see the shapes of what looked like jars of Betty's jams and chutneys stacked in the recess under the stairs on one side. That would account for the smell. On his other side, only darkness.

Peering closer, he realised he was precariously perched at the top of a steep set of stone steps. He shrank away from the drop as the tickle in his nose intensified.

Eyes watering and pinching his nose tightly, Fletcher stretched one tentative foot onto the first step. If he could get down to the cellar, perhaps he could sneeze into the handkerchief without being heard. It would also provide a bit more breathing space until they were able to get out of that blasted house of horrors.

Moving as slowly and quietly as possible, he crept to the second step as the sound of cupboards opening and closing, and pans banging about in the kitchen grew louder. Reaching back, he tugged on the hem of May's dress and gestured below. After a moment's hesitation, she turned and followed him down.

Amazingly, the scent of vinegar grew even stronger as they descended. In the pitch black, Fletcher bumped into what sounded like a box of glass jars. They clinked together just as music started upstairs. Betty had turned on the radio. May and Fletcher froze, raising their heads to listen for footsteps overhead until it seemed the coast was clear.

'It looks like she's doing some more baking,' May whispered, pulling her phone from her handbag and switching on the torch. 'We may be here a while.'

The light revealed jars of mincemeat stacked around the bottom of the stairs and a washer and dryer against one wall, piled high with musty-smelling laundry. Only darkness stretched away from them towards the front of the house.

'That's just perfect,' Fletcher replied, still feeling touchy. 'Are we supposed to stay down here until she goes to bed? What if she can't sleep again? Do we stay down here, eating pickles and shitting in the corner until she finally leaves the house again? Or maybe we just live here now. I call dibs on this end of the cellar. At least I'll be able to wash my fucking clothes when they get dirty. Not that it'll matter, since absolutely everything stinks of vinegar anyway.'

May turned to look directly at him. The torch cast ghoulish shadows across her face. In the dank cellar, he almost felt afraid of her. 'Are you quite finished?' she said.

The tickle in his nose started up again. He began to inhale with an 'Ah... ah... ah...'

May put her phone in his hand and propelled him further into the darkness. 'For fuck's sake, get as far away as possible if you're going to sneeze,' she said.

Fletcher took the phone, pinched his nose with the handkerchief and made his way quickly but carefully through the maze of rickety shelves and precarious boxes to the other end of the cellar. The scent seemed to become stronger still back there. He peered at the floor in the darkness, using the phone's torch as a spotlight, but there was no sign of a spilled jar.

Reaching the front wall he found a doorway, leading to what he assumed was the coal hole. Most houses of a certain age have a small bunker at one end of the cellar, directly under the front door, made for storing coal. A small hole with a metal cover, like a mini manhole, is situated on the pavement in front of the house, allowing easy delivery without sooty bags being carried through the home. The coal hole would be the perfect place for Fletcher to finally allow himself to sneeze.

As he made his way through the narrow brick archway, the itch in his nose began to increase in anticipation. Using the phone's light, he made out an enormous, rusty claw-foot bathtub wedged into the opposite end of the bunker. The pungent scent of vinegar was overwhelming and mixed with something meaty and sweetish. Fletcher made his way towards the tub, getting as far from the kitchen end of the cellar as possible. He would have one satisfying sneeze, then work out how to get out of this reeking Black Hole of Calcutta as quickly as possible.

He was building up with a satisfying 'ah... ah... ah...' for a sneeze that never materialised. All breath left Fletcher's body in a sudden wheeze of shock as the light from May's phone revealed the grim contents of the stinking tub.

CHAPTER FORTY-ONE

SPLISH SPLASH

May watched as the torch on her phone bobbed away from her as Fletcher made his way to the other end of the cellar. They really were in a pickle. And surrounded by them too, if the smell was anything to go by. It could be hours before Betty went out again or decided to go to bed. Where was that damn key?

Betty had said it was on a hook in her kitchen. The hooks were there, but no key fob. Had she hidden it somewhere in the house after May had asked to borrow it? Was she keeping it in her handbag? If it was in Betty's bag, May felt certain she would be able to get her hands on it. She just needed the right opportunity. If Betty would just go out again, May would take a closer look through that kitchen. She hadn't even had a chance to look through the drawers before Betty came home. Or the hall table. That was a likely place to store a spare key.

The phone light bobbed back towards her through the darkness, returning much faster than it had left. She hadn't heard Fletcher's sneeze. At least that was one good thing.

Fletcher arrived panting, grasping her arm with a shaking hand as he whispered incoherently in her ear.

May pulled her head away and tried to release herself from the clawing grip he had on her arm. 'What are you trying to say?' she hissed. 'You're just spitting in my ear.' She rubbed at the side of her face.

Fletcher bowed his head, took a deep breath and swallowed, before trying again.

'What happened to Betty's husband?' he asked.

Betty's husband? What on earth was he on about?

'He died,' May said. 'When they were on holiday. In Spain, I think.'

'Did you ever see the body? Go to his funeral?' Fletcher said.

'No,' she said, exasperated. It was not the time for village gossip. 'I never saw his body. He was buried up north somewhere. In a family plot, I believe.'

Fletcher looked over his shoulder, back into the gloom. 'I think he's in the tub,' he said.

Christ, was he having an episode of some sort? The stress of the situation getting to him?

'He's dead,' she said, enunciating each word as much as possible while continuing to whisper. 'He's not taking a bath. He died. *Died.*'

Fletcher shook his head and pointed to the other end of the cellar. Then grabbed her arm and dragged her forward.

As they silently crept towards the darkest part of the cellar, Fletcher's grip on her arm vibrated with tension. At the entrance to the coal hole he stopped, put the phone in her hand, took her handbag and motioned for her to enter.

'Are you not coming?' she asked.

'I've seen enough already,' he replied with a shiver, positioning himself outside the archway.

May paused as her brain sorted through the complicated stench surrounding them.

The standard earthy scent of a cellar.

Vinegar. For the pickles.

Fruit. For the jam.

And... something else. Something musky and revolting. Like a butcher shop.

Meat.

Oh.

Oh, dear.

She shuffled through the doorway towards a large, metal tub at the other end of the space, already certain of what she would find there.

Holding her phone up, the light shone down on the murky liquid. Two milky eyes looked up at her, a mouth gaped open in a silent scream, dark hair floated in a halo around the pale face, emphasising the disturbing dent in the middle of his forehead. The head was surrounded by floating wedges of onion, cloves of garlic, peppercorns, bay leaves and what looked like mustard seeds.

'Ophelia's got nothing on him,' Fletcher said at May's shoulder, causing her to flinch.

She turned to him, relieved to see his reassuring face after staring at the miserable remains of Chester Danvers. 'I thought you were going to wait outside,' she said.

'It's creepy out there in the dark all alone,' he replied.

'And it's bloody Disneyland in here, is it?' She turned back to the tub.

Gesturing towards the body he continued, 'What do you think happened? That's a nasty wound on his forehead. Do you think Betty did it?'

May shrugged. 'He didn't pickle himself. She must be involved in some way.'

'And what's happened to the rest of him?' Fletcher whispered. Where Millais's *Ophelia* is wearing a white dress flowing in the currents of the river where she drowned, there were only scraggly bits floating in the tub's murky liquid. Remnants at which May chose not to look too closely.

'I put him in the mincemeat,' Betty Danvers said from the entrance to the coal hole.

May and Fletcher jumped at the voice in the gloom. May fumbled with her phone. The light spun in the air, creating an incongruous disco effect, before dropping into the filthy tub and plunging them into absolute darkness.

CHAPTER FORTY-TWO

I'VE GOT YOU UNDER MY SKIN

The overhead fluorescents came on with a snap, blinding May and Fletcher with the sudden brightness.

'Might as well turn the lights on,' Betty said, still standing in the doorway. 'I'm so sorry you had to see the house in such a state. It's been a difficult few months.'

'That's perfectly understandable,' May replied, squinting at her across the coal bunker.

'First Mum, then Chester. It's been a bloody nightmare to be honest.' Betty sounded oddly like her usual self, as if they were discussing the weather in the bookshop, not standing beside what remained of her dead husband fermenting in a vinegar bath in the cellar.

'I'm sure you understand,' she said to May. 'Adjusting to life without a partner is awful, though of course you still have your lovely mum. It's been a trying time what with Mary on the other side of the world and me here on my own dealing with all of this.'

Betty nodded towards the tub. 'I didn't know what to do with him. With Mum it was so nice and tidy. They took her away and I stripped the bed and had it all cleaned up by that afternoon. You'd never know someone had died there.' She shook her head with regret. 'Chester was a different story. I couldn't explain the state of him, of his...' she touched her own forehead, '...so I had to deal with it myself. Getting a body down the cellar steps isn't easy.'

'Depends on how you go about it,' Fletcher said.

May glanced at him, then back to Betty. 'Go on,' she said. Betty sounded like she needed to talk it out.

'I'd heard that lye can be used to... you know.' She wrinkled her nose in disgust. 'But I had no reason to be buying lye. I didn't want to draw attention to myself by buying big sacks of the stuff at the DIY store and having the whole village wondering what I was up to. I thought about making soaps as a cover or doing some DIY in the garden. I've always fancied a nice patio.' She wrinkled her nose again. 'But I'm a baker at heart, not a soap-maker, and laying a patio is something Chester would do, not me. Then I remembered my grandmother's recipe for Christmas mincemeat made with beef. It was exactly the right time to be buying lemons and spice, raisins and apples and glacé cherries. No one would raise an eyebrow if I had a trolley full of those things, so...' She looked down at the remains of Chester in the bathtub.

'You ate him?' Fletcher said, eyes wide, thinking of the jars of pickles and mincemeat in the cellar.

Betty made a face. 'Don't be disgusting. Of course I didn't eat him. *You* did.'

Fletcher made a sound like a horse whinnying and sat down on the edge of the tub, then he remembered what was in the tub and tried to stand up again. In the end, he braced himself with one hand against the stony wall.

'Just breathe,' May said, gently pressing him to sit back down, regardless of what was floating right behind him. Fletcher placed his buttocks on the very edge of the tub and bent forward, keeping his face as far away from Chester's remains as possible.

May looked at Betty again. 'You put him in jars of mincemeat? The ones you gave everyone in the village as Christmas gifts?' Revolting, but as a means of body disposal it was bloody brilliant.

Fletcher retched violently in his hunched-over position.

Betty blushed and pursed her lips together as she nodded. 'And the mincemeat pies I made for the Christmas service... and the ones you sold in the bookshop. And the cakes we sold at the Christmas fair. And the hot cross buns I've been giving away all month. Chester was quite a big man.'

Fletcher groaned. 'I think I might faint,' he said, grasping May's leg for support.

'Just keep breathing,' she replied, resting her hand on the back of his head. 'In through the nose, out through the mouth.'

Fletcher sounded like he was preparing to give birth as he huffed and puffed in the small space.

'It was all properly cooked,' Betty snapped. 'There was no danger of food poisoning or anything like that. I would never do anything to harm anyone.'

Fletcher stopped panting long enough to look up at Betty then towards the bathtub.

Betty tutted. 'Well, apart from that obviously.'

'And your mother?' May asked, buying time. She scanned the bunker for a weapon, but apart from the tub, the room was empty. Fletcher must've left her handbag outside. If May could get to it, she had one of her blades stashed inside. She cursed the flimsy spring dress she was wearing and its lack of pockets or hiding places.

At the mention of her mother, Betty seemed to wilt. She sagged against the door frame. 'Mum was ill for so long. I can't remember a time when she wasn't suffering with one thing or another, but the doctors could never find anything wrong with her. Charlatans, every last one of them.' She looked up with fierce eyes. For the first time, May could see the madness reflected in them. 'She trusted no one but me, but I couldn't be with her *all the time*. It was an impossible situation.' She started to cry. 'I miss her so much.'

'I'm so sorry, Betty,' May said. There were no windows in the coal bunker, only the small opening in the ceiling, which was sealed up.

'I couldn't care for Mum *and* Chester *and* work *and* bake *and* run the church volunteers. I had to make a choice,' Betty said.

'Of course you did,' May said gently. Betty was blocking the only exit. If May and Fletcher were going to get out of there, they'd have to go through her.

Fletcher had recovered some composure and staggered upright to stand beside May. 'You killed your own mother?' he blurted. May gripped his arm, willing him to shut up.

'No!' Betty shook her head, suddenly spitting with rage. 'I would *never* do anything like that. I just released her from her pain. She was suffering and I made it stop. That's all.'

May had an iron grip on his wrist, but Fletcher couldn't seem to stop himself. 'Couldn't the police tell you'd... released her?' he asked.

'Of course not,' Betty said. 'I'm a nurse.' She rolled her eyes. 'Mum had been under a doctor's care for years. Everyone knew she was ill. There was no post-mortem. She just died. That's what everyone believed.' She stood up straight again and took a deep breath. 'Except Chester.'

'Ah,' May said, looking down at the disagreeably departed.

'He said he was going to go to the police. Said I'd committed *murder*.' Betty laughed in a way that chilled May to the bone. 'He wouldn't let it go. I'd inherited Mum's house and a bit of money when she passed, but he said if I signed it all over to him, he'd keep my dirty secret.'

'So you killed him,' Fletcher said, clearly unable to control himself.

'No! I gave him everything. Everything except Mum's wedding ring.' She rubbed the tiny gold band on one finger. 'It was the only thing I wanted to keep, but Chester wouldn't hear of it. He wanted it all, including the ring. We argued. I explained that it wasn't worth much and I offered to pay him even more than it was worth, but he just wouldn't see sense.' Betty sighed and shrugged her shoulders in defeat. 'That's when I killed him.'

May nodded. She'd always found Chester Danvers to be a pompous, controlling arse of a man. It was surprisingly gratifying to have her assessment confirmed. She took enormous satisfaction in his grisly comeuppance. To be fair, May would've preferred not to have digested the man. The thought of any part of him inside her own body was abhorrent, but what was done was done.

'Come, Betty,' May said. 'Let's go upstairs and talk this through.' If May could just get to her handbag...

Fletcher was suddenly alert with the possibility of escape in sight. 'Yes, a cup of tea would go down a treat right about now.'

Betty frowned, her eyes full of sadness. 'I'm so sorry,' she said, picking up a rusty machete that had been propped outside the archway. Its sharpened blade reflected glints of light from the overhead bulbs. 'I know I'm being a very poor hostess, but I'm afraid I can't let you leave.'

CHAPTER FORTY-THREE

IT'S THE SAME OLD SONG

'Wait!' Fletcher shouted, as Betty started to advance towards them, machete raised above her head. 'What about the dogs? What have you done with them?'

'Seriously?' Betty lowered the knife, halting her progress across the small space. 'I'm about to cut you in half and you want to know about the bloody dogs?'

Fletcher glanced at May, who seemed frozen in place. 'Yes,' he said. 'My dying wish is to know what you've done with Bess and George.'

Betty shrugged. 'They're at my mum's house. They're fine. Do you know what I can get for them online? It's an absolute travesty what some fools will pay for a stupid *dog*.'

Fletcher sensed a flash of movement beside him, then Betty was on the ground, both hands at her own throat as she gasped for air. May was standing over her, furious with indignation.

'You absolute bitch,' May said. 'Don't you dare disparage Bess and George. Those two little angels bring nothing but joy wherever they go. You can threaten to kill me, you can stab Fletcher in the back–'

'Steady on,' Fletcher said.

'–but you leave my dogs the fuck alone.' May picked up the machete and raised it over her head with both hands. Fletcher closed his eyes and turned away just as the cellar door thumped open and two police officers rushed down the stone steps.

Much later, May, Fletcher, Minty, Sparks, Bastian and Erika gathered in the library. Fletcher had showered twice but swore he could still smell vinegar. His new suit had gone straight into the bin.

Fletcher stood at the entrance to the library, his phone in his hand. Satoshi had texted the results of the DNA test hours before, but Fletcher had been too occupied to read them. Now that he knew for sure, he had to decide what to do with the information.

May was curled up in an armchair, hair still damp from her shower, two contented dachshunds snoozing on each side of her. They'd been checked over by Beresford, the village vet, and declared perfectly fine after their little adventure. May was wearing the lovely cashmere sweats Fletcher had bought her and looked cosy and radiant as she sipped her martini.

Fletcher set his phone on the shelf in the niche outside the library. His discussion with May could wait.

Bastian was shaking his head. 'I can't believe it was Betty this whole time. She certainly changed after her mother died, but I thought she was blossoming, not going mad.'

Erika sat beside him, sipping a cranberry juice. She seemed happy just to be there, following the conversation from person to person as if she was watching a tennis match.

'How did you stop her?' Sparks asked. 'It sounds like you were in a pretty tight situation down in that cellar.' He looked at Fletcher with concern. Fletcher felt his insides melt.

'I just punched her in the throat,' May replied. *'Krav maga.* Can't beat it when it comes to self-defence. So efficient, no faffing about.'

'That's my girl,' Minty piped up. 'To crap mega, or whatever it is you said.' She held up her glass in a toast.

'To crap mega!' Everyone toasted.

May turned to Minty. 'What made you call the police? We didn't even suspect Betty this afternoon.'

Minty preened, enjoying her moment in the spotlight. 'I overheard someone on the heath talking about Jilly going off to Magaluf with Humphrey Oslac's widow, Muriel. Apparently, they'd had a thing for years but were so secretive about it that even someone called Darcy didn't know.' She shrugged. 'Then I realised it probably wasn't Jilly who'd taken the dogs if she was all loved up in Spain. Then Betty started behaving oddly, getting angry over nothing. That's when it clicked. It's those patterns, you see. Betty's grandmother killed her grandfather, never proven of course, but everyone knew.' She sipped her drink. 'Blood will always tell. That's when I realised it could be Betty behind it all, so I rang the police on Erika's mobile telephone and reported a murder.'

Fletcher spluttered into his G&T. 'You reported a murder? No wonder those coppers were so quick on the scene. What they walked into must've been far worse than their wildest expectations.' He tried to imagine the gruesome tableau they'd presented with Betty on the floor and May standing over her, machete raised, Fletcher in shock, the remains of Chester in the bath. It beggared belief.

'Well, I wasn't wrong,' Minty pointed out. 'I didn't *know* she'd killed her husband. I just thought she might be dangerous. If I'd tried to explain the whole complicated reason why I was calling, the police would've arrived too late, if at all.'

Fletcher winked at May. 'I think we would've been all right,' he said. 'But thank you for your quick thinking, Minty.'

'Did Betty explain about the text messages?' Bastian asked.

May tried to shift position, causing the dogs to grumble. She settled back into place. 'Betty explained about *everything*. They couldn't get her to *stop* talking. It must've been agony for her to keep such a big secret for so many months.'

'She said her mother never approved of David and Juan.' Fletcher sniffed. 'She always thought their relationship was a sin against God. Particularly so with David being a vicar. It was the same with the rest of the messages, all people doing things of which her mother did not approve.'

'Sounds as if she went a bit Norman Bates towards the end,' Minty added. 'I don't remember her grandmother ever doing that. Lizzie was a nasty bitch, but she wasn't doolally.'

'What about the Shakespeare?' Sparks asked. 'Was there a reason for those in the text messages?'

'That seems to be about her father,' May replied. 'He taught English at the comprehensive and loved Shakespeare. Remember the two messages that didn't include initials? They were a kind of confession on her part, about killing Chester and essentially feeding him to the village.'

'They *were* delicious buns,' Minty said, as everyone groaned.

'Don't,' Fletcher replied. 'My stomach has only just settled down.'

'Speaking of the messages,' May said. 'Was there one this morning? I haven't seen it and my phone was taken as evidence along with the rest of Chester's tub of horrors.'

'Yep, there was and it was a cracker,' Bastian said. 'She must've sent it on the heath just before she left. I received it in the book stall along with a bunch of other people.'

'I got it too,' Erika said, pleased to be included.

Bastian went to retrieve his mobile from the niche outside the library, then paused on the threshold and looked to May for permission to bring it in.

'Go on then,' she said.

'I feel like I should be bursting into flames with this in here,' he said, smiling at May as he reclaimed his seat. Bastian tapped at the screen. 'Here we go. Looks like this one was for me.'

He held up the phone as everyone leaned forward to read.

Give him diseases, leaving with him his lust.
You get what you deserve. SL

CHAPTER FORTY-FOUR

GOODNIGHT, SWEETHEART

Minty was sitting up in bed listening to Duke Ellington when May took in her Horlicks. 'What a day,' she said, as May set the cup and saucer on the cabinet in front of her portrait. 'Murder, mayhem and a misbegotten daughter. I can't wait to see what happens tomorrow.'

May looked at the photograph of a young Minty and, for the first time, it didn't irritate her. She understood why Minty might want to hold on to some part of her youth. For a brief moment that afternoon in the cellar, May had felt real fear. She'd felt the genuine vulnerability of her age when Betty raised that big knife. It had been a quick flash of terror before the rage rushed in to take its place, but that flash had been enough. It had knocked the breath out of her, leaving her frozen and helpless. She decided to find a new *krav maga* instructor as soon as possible. And make sure that in the future, all her dresses had pockets.

'I guess things will return to normal now,' Minty said, with a sigh.

May moved a chair to sit beside the bed. 'Don't sound so disappointed, this *is* normal for Blackheath.' She looked at her mother. 'But you don't have to worry about that, do you? I thought you were dying soon?'

Minty sipped her Horlicks. 'I may stick around a bit longer, just to keep you on your toes. Erika seems like a dear. I'd like to arrange that party for her. Do you know anything about her mother?'

'The only thing I know is that she and Bastian met when they were both working for a circus in Djibouti. She was an acrobat; he was the ringmaster. It sounds like one of Barb's novels,' May said. 'If you want more details, ask Erika. Bastian is notoriously tight-lipped when it comes to his past.'

'What did Betty mean by that last message about Bastian?' Minty asked.

May chuckled. 'It seems Betty has a tendency to draw the wrong conclusions. That MM message was directed at me after she saw the condom in the bin on one of her visits here. She used arsenic-laced rat poison from her mother's house and put it in the Horlicks tin, to punish me for being such a harlot, when really you were the harlot.'

Minty gave her a warning look, then held up her cup. 'This Horlicks, I assume.'

'I think I can come up with something better than that to poison you with,' May said.

'Right,' Minty replied. 'So, does Bastian have syphilis or not?'

'He gets a lot of ear infections because of his achondroplasia,' May continued.

'His what?' Minty asked.

May waved her hands, annoyed at the interruption. 'It's what caused his dwarfism,' she said. 'Betty must've noticed that he was taking antibiotics and drew her own, incorrect, conclusions about a sexually transmitted disease.'

'Mind in the gutter,' Minty said, taking another sip.

'Dangerously so,' May replied. 'She'd put rat poison in Bastian's green tea. Thankfully, like us, he'd had the sense to clear things out after he saw the message. We only know about the attempted poisonings because of Betty's very detailed confession.'

Minty looked at the mug in her hand. 'This would be an opportune moment for you to get rid of me. It could all be blamed on Betty. Shame you didn't think of that.'

'Who says I didn't?' May replied with a smile.

Minty finished her drink then set the empty cup in its saucer on the bedside cabinet. 'As long as they can't trace it back to you,' she said. 'I'd hate for you to go down for my murder.'

'Don't be daft,' May replied.

Minty snuggled down against the pillows. 'I've had a lovely life,' she said. 'Not perfect, but I suspect perfect would've been rather boring.' She looked at May. 'You're a good girl, Polly May. You have a good heart. I know I wasn't the mother you needed, but somehow you've turned out surprisingly well. Not perfect, but–'

'Perfect would've been rather boring,' May finished for her.

'I was going to say, not perfect, but close enough.' Minty stuck out her tongue, then smiled.

May looked at Minty's portrait. 'Fletcher was in a tizz this evening about something that I'd like to discuss with you,' she said.

'That sounds ominous,' Minty replied. She folded her hands over the duvet. 'Fire away.'

May took a deep breath. 'He got it into his head that Bertie wasn't my real father.' May saw Minty flinch from the corner of her eye. 'In fact, he was convinced that my father was actually Mordecai Page.'

'Mordecai Page! I never. How could Fletcher think that I would ever–' Minty was pink with indignation.

'He proved himself wrong,' May said, holding up her hands in surrender. 'He actually broke into Mordecai's house for a DNA sample and sent it off with some hair from my hairbrush for a paternity test.'

'Fletcher did that?' Minty said.

May nodded. 'He stole Mordecai's toothbrush, and he was damn proud of it. Never underestimate Fletch when he gets a bee in his bonnet. The test proved that Mordecai wasn't my father, but I don't think Bertie was either. Was he?'

Minty shook her head slowly. She extracted the locket from the collar of her nightgown and opened it. 'This is your father,' she said.

May looked at the image of a young man in uniform. She saw her own slim nose and high forehead reflected in his face. 'Did you love him?' she asked.

Minty closed her eyes. 'More than anything,' she replied.

'Why didn't you tell me?' May asked. Part of her admired Minty for keeping the secret for so long, but part of her was furious. 'Bertie died forty years ago. What did it matter?'

Minty sighed. 'I suppose I felt I owed it to Bertie. He was a decent man in his own way, just an unhappy one. It might be hard to believe, but he loved you more than he loved anyone. I thought about telling you many times, but I couldn't see what difference it would make.' She looked away. 'Of course, that was just me avoiding all those messy, difficult emotions.'

May studied the photo of her father. 'What was his name? I'm assuming he's dead.'

'Yes,' Minty said. 'That was the problem. He died when I was carrying you. We weren't yet married, my parents were in a state, and there was Bertie offering to marry me and raise you as his own. He was even happy to take the Morrigan name. I was virtually catatonic with grief. The next thing I knew, I was a wife and mother. My life had been decided for me.' Minty swallowed. 'His name was Frank. Frank Parker.' There was a catch in her voice. 'I haven't said his name out loud since you were born.'

'Does Cass know?' May asked.

Minty shook her head. 'Of course not. I wouldn't tell one of you without telling the other. You can give her all the details when she comes here.'

May looked at Minty. 'What do you mean? Cass hasn't been to England in decades. Why should she come now?'

'I think she'll come to her own mother's funeral, if only to make sure I'm well and truly dead,' Minty replied. 'Castor Kay and Pollux May, together again.' She chuckled at the look of horror on May's face. 'God help us all. I almost wish I was going to be here to see it.' Minty continued to smile as she closed her eyes. She sighed deeply one last time before gently slipping away.

May Morrigan sat in the darkness beside her mother's bed for a very long time.

EPILOGUE
THIS WILL BE OUR YEAR

May adjusted the little black hat with its full veil. It had been a splurge, purchased just for the occasion. The hat was a touch over the top (well, more than a touch) but she would have appreciated the effort. The black gloves and wool dress were becoming itchy in the rising warmth of the morning. May used her Kelly handbag as a shield to scratch discreetly. Summer had arrived in London.

Fletcher stood beside her in his dark suit and tie, set off with a slash of red lipstick and crimson nails. He looked dazed and tearful. 'I can't believe she's really gone,' he said. 'The house will feel so empty without her.'

Sparks squeezed his shoulder. 'She was a remarkable woman. One of a kind.'

'She'll be dearly missed,' Bastian said, bowing his head. 'But she leaves a remarkable legacy behind.'

They formed a small circle in front of the new memorial stone. Bess and George, wearing black bows for the occasion, snuffled in the grass beside the grave. Fletcher raised his head and gazed around at the glory of Highgate Cemetery. 'You did well, getting a spot here,' he said to May. 'She would love this.'

He began to cry in earnest, turning his face into Sparks's shoulder.

'I loved her very much,' May whispered, holding back tears. 'I can't believe I'll never see her again.'

'Oh, for the love of Pete,' Minty squawked. 'What did you bury? A leopard-print kaftan and a bottle of Chanel No 5?'

May sighed. 'Barb was a very important part of our lives. This is our chance to say goodbye properly. She deserves a decent send-off.'

Minty rolled her eyes but remained blessedly silent.

They all turned back towards the memorial which read:

Barbara Brigitte Bouvier

Novelist, Friend, Lover

Forever the Life & Soul

Bastian reached into his satchel and pulled out a glass. Kneeling, he set it down on the stone, then extracted a cocktail shaker and a small plastic container from the bag. He poured a perfect G&T, garnishing it with juniper berries and a slice of lemon.

'I hope you have enough for all of us,' Minty said.

'Just for Barb,' Bastian replied, standing and raising an imaginary glass. 'To Barbara Bouvier.'

The others raised their hands in a toast.

'And all our yesterdays–' Bastian began.

'No Shakespeare, *please!*' May protested. The others nodded in agreement.

Bastian paused a moment before continuing. 'Strike hands with me, the glasses brim. The dew is on the heather. For love is good and life is long. And friends are best together.'

'Here, here,' Sparks said.

'I'd like to say something,' Minty piped up.

May suppressed a groan.

'I didn't know Barb well,' Minty continued, 'but I saw the happy effect her existence had on two young people whom I love dearly...'

May reached out to take Fletcher's hand.

'...and for that I will be eternally grateful.' Minty nodded. 'Now, children, someone needs to buy me a drink before I expire from dehydration. I hear vodka is very refreshing.'

The group shuffled out through the spectacular entrance to the cemetery, a solemn clique in their funereal black. Even the dogs seemed to sense the seriousness of the occasion and were on their best behaviour.

Bastian was especially blue since Erika had returned to her mother's house, but she had promised to visit Blackheath again soon. Minty's baby shower to celebrate Erika's arrival had been a huge success. They'd covered Greenway's garden in pink bunting and Minty had arranged for a hunky stripper, dressed as a baby, to jump out of a huge pink cake. It had been a day no one would soon forget.

On that sad day at Highgate Cemetery, Fletcher was absolutely glowing. The newspapers had quickly lost interest in Barb's story when a popular soap star was exposed for having an affair with his own step-sister. Once the journalists had faded into the woodwork, Fletcher realised that the whole experience had caused him to reassess his life and he had decided to make some big changes. Saying goodbye to Barb was one of them.

He'd started a new book, in his own name for the first time. It was an international gay romance, and his agent was ecstatic. The genre was booming. Fletcher and Sparks were planning a research trip to Paris in a few weeks. They would visit the Louvre, stroll through the Marais and eat croissants every day.

May was certain this new chapter in his life would be his best yet.

Fletcher had found love and had big plans for his future. But what about May?

She knew her own future was less certain. There was a battle ahead over her divorce settlement but May relished the opportunity to see James in court. She hadn't laid eyes on him since he'd walked out of her life. Would he dare to fight her for Greenway? Just let him try.

For the first time in a very long time, May felt strong and hopeful about the future. Perhaps she would even go on a date that summer. A certain delicious-smelling, locksmith/artist immediately sprang to mind. May felt an unexpected thrill at the thought of him.

It looked like Minty was going to stick around a bit longer, if only to make sure May went on that date. Minty had become slightly less annoying as she started to make new friends at Blackheath's Age Exchange, organising a regular poker night for the members at Greenway. It gave May a taste of what it might have been like to raise a rowdy teenager.

As they waited to cross Swain's Lane, a small hand slipped into May's.

'Don't want you to get hit by a car,' Minty said, watching the traffic and giving May's hand a squeeze.

May smiled. The lights changed and they all crossed the road together.

THE END

ALSO BY KATHERINE BLACK

A Most Unusual Demise

ACKNOWLEDGEMENTS

My second book, what an incredible dream come true. I am so enjoying this new adventure as a writer. Huge thanks to Betsy Reavley and Fred Freeman at Bloodhound Books for their support and encouragement. Monumental thanks to my lovely editor, Ian Skewis, for his patience, guidance, and much needed hand-holding. Unlike my first book, which was workshopped and graded at UEA over a span of two years, this book was written in four months with only Ian seeing it once it was 'finished'. (Those quote marks are working very hard indeed.) Thank you so much, Ian. I'm very grateful.

Thanks, as always, to the gorgeous friends who keep me laughing and moving forward: Jenny, Kellie and Nikki: love you, love you, love you. I hope you know it.

Jacquie, Jo, Jean, Katie, Natasha, Poppy, Pippa, Rachel, Sarah C, Sarah D: so many coffees, so many cakes, so much laughter and so many tears in the last year. Thank you for making sure the laughter always outweighs the tears.

Thanks to Matt and everyone at Halcyon Books in Lee for hosting my weekly Shut Up and Write! group. And thanks to everyone who's come for a quiet hour of writing with me. There were busy weeks when it was the only hour I managed to get the words down. Thanks for keeping me accountable and special thanks to Matt for keeping the ice machine going.

Thank you to my lovely family (especially Rosie) for putting up with my odd hours, weird questions and very, very occasionally grumpy attitude during the writing of this book.

May and Fletcher will be back later this year in a Christmas adventure. Bring on the mince pies!

Listen to the *A Most Malicious Messenger* playlist on Spotify.

For updates, bonus chapters and more, join the mailing list at kjblack.com.

A NOTE FROM THE PUBLISHER

Thank you for reading this book. If you enjoyed it please do consider leaving a review on Amazon to help others find it too.

We hate typos. All of our books have been rigorously edited and proofread, but sometimes mistakes do slip through. If you have spotted a typo, please do let us know and we can get it amended within hours.

info@bloodhoundbooks.com

Made in the USA
Columbia, SC
02 February 2024

31358296R00150